MAIZE AND MONSTERS

Author: Tom Knauss

Project Managers: Zach Glazar and Tom Knauss

Editor: Jeff Harkness

Swords & Wizardry Rules Conversion: Jeff Harkness

Art Direction: Casey Christofferson

Layout and Graphic Design: Charles A. Wright

Cover Design: Charles A. Wright

Cover Art: Héctor Rodríguez Antúnez

Interior Art: Héctor Rodríguez Antúnez

Cartography: Robert Altbauer

©2020 Frog God Games. All rights reserved. Reproduction without the written permission of the publisher is expressly forbidden. Frog God Games and the Frog God Games logo is a trademark of Frog God Games. All characters, names, places, items, art and text herein are copyrighted by Frog God Games, Inc. The mention of or reference to any company or product in these pages is not a challenge to the trademark or copyright concerned.

Product Identity: The following items are hereby identified as Frog God Games LLC's Product Identity, as defined in the Open Game License version 1.0a, Section 1(e), and are not Open Game Content: product and product line names, logos and identifying marks including trade dress; artifacts; creatures; characters; stories, storylines, plots, thematic elements, dialogue, incidents, language, artwork, symbols, designs, depictions, likenesses, formats, poses, concepts, themes and graphic, photographic and other visual or audio representations; names and descriptions of characters, spells, enchantments, personalities, teams, personas, likenesses and sptecial abilities; places, locations, environments, creatures, equipment, magical or supernatural abilities or effects, logos, symbols, or graphic designs; and any other trademark or registered trademark clearly identified as Product Identity. Previously released Open Game Content is excluded from the above list.

ADVENTURES
WORTH
WINNING

FROG GOD GAMES

ISBN:978-1-943067-55-8

FROG GOD GAMES IS:

Bill Webb, Matthew J. Finch, Zach Glazar, Charles A. Wright, Edwin Nagy, Mike Badolato, John Barnhouse

Table of Contents

MAIZE AND MONSTERS

"PLANTS NOURISHED WITH FOULED WATER CAN STILL FEED A VILLAGE.
A GRAIN OF SAND POISONED WITH THE BLOOD OF INNOCENTS CAN KILL A CITY."

— AN AZTLI PROVERB

Maize and Monsters is an adventure for 4th- to 6th-level characters that exposes the adventurers to the grim reality that time sometimes exacerbates old wounds rather than healing them. A recent murder in the village of Pilhua proves to be far more than a simple crime of passion as the seeds for this killing were sown during a previous, unsolved mystery that still haunts some residents within the settlement. The characters must wade through a list of suspects and motives that lead them to discover the ugly truth about a heinous crime that spawned a greater evil than even its perpetrators could ever imagine.

ADVENTURE BACKGROUND

In the Caya Grasslands of northern Tehuatl, most people's lives revolve around the cultivation and harvesting of maize. The crop feeds much of the population and is considered by most to be the lifeblood of society. While the cereal grain usually stands as a silent witness to humanity's actions, there are rare occasions where the stain of evil compels the mindless, green stalks to step forward and provide their irrefutable testimony to man's heinousness.

A little more than one year ago, Conto and his younger sister Chipinia spent a lazy afternoon lying in the maizefields just outside their village staring at the clouds moving across the skies. Away from their parents' attentive gaze, the teenagers enjoyed a brief respite of freedom in the seldom visited, remote locale just beyond the outskirts of their settlement, where they indulged in smoking some tobacco and drinking pulque. Unfortunately, the youngsters were not the only ones that day who wished to go unseen and unnoticed. Two local pochtecas named Mixoch and Temilaz had spent the last several years cultivating a lucrative business relationship with Uetzopilli, a Poqoza from south of the Great Canal who smuggles psychedelic mushrooms and other hallucinogens into the village for distribution throughout the area. The wily half-elf excelled at eluding the authorities and hiding his contraband, but the shady and untrustworthy peddler also had a penchant for swindling his customers and making unnecessary enemies.

During his previous visit north of the waterway separating the island, Uetzopilli had sold worthless, rotting mushrooms to the unscrupulous merchants for a handsome price. The slight proved too much for the pair to ignore after their commercial partner's previous shortcomings and false promises had worn their patience to the bone. The duo naturally hid their displeasure and lured Uetzopilli back to their village under the pretense of partaking in another profitable deal with him. When he arrived at the rendezvous site outside their village, Mixoch and Temilaz's handiwork awaited him. After a few minutes of idle banter and chatter, the startled Uetzopilli quickly came to the realization that something was terribly amiss as he spoke with the duo who were resting their weary arms on their uictlis. When the two men stepped forward, the half-elf suddenly found himself staring into the gaping hole they had dug in the isolated maizefield before his anticipated arrival. In his dangerous line of work, even the naïve Uetzopilli knew what came next, but an unexpected surprise awaited the three conspirators.

The argument and pleas for mercy roused the two youngsters from their tenuous slumber and beckoned them to investigate the transaction further. At first, the teenagers prudently remained quiet and still. However, when the vicious Mixoch thrust his tecpatl into Uetzopilli's abdomen and punctured his heart, the siblings simultaneously shrieked in horror. The shocked murderers momentarily stared at the children's scared faces and instinctually realized the steps they must take to maintain their silence. The wicked pair instantly recognized Conto and Chipinia from the village, and the frightened siblings also knew the killers' identities, marking them for death as well. The panicked 15- and 14-year-olds froze in their tracks, giving Mixoch and Temilaz ample opportunity to pounce on their tragic, innocent witnesses and quickly slay them like livestock for slaughter. The two criminals also tossed their limp, lifeless bodies into the hole along with Mixoch's broken tecpatl and frantically shoveled dirt back into the abscess as if despoiled earth could erase the stains of their sins from the land. The bloodletting lasted less than one minute, but within those 60 seconds, the devious pochtecas had sown the seeds for the terror that would later befall the village.

Naturally, Conto and Chipinia's disappearance prompted an outcry from the children's distraught family and fellow villagers, but an exhaustive search revealed nothing. Mixoch and Temilaz covered their tracks well, at least for now. Evidence of their gruesome crimes eluded investigators, and as days dragged into weeks and then into months, the terrible memories faded and life returned to normal for almost everyone except the children's grieving immediate family members. Yet the secluded gravesite and its occupants refused to rest in peace. The children's innocent blood gave birth to and fed a fearsome terror that soon took root in the increasingly overgrown maizefield. One year later, Conto and Chipinia's restless spirits awoke from their uneasy slumber and plunged their homeland into despair.

ADVENTURE SYNOPSIS

The characters arrive in the small Aztli village of Pilhua in the southern portion of the Caya Grasslands roughly 80 miles due north of the central causeway spanning the Great Canal. One year has passed since the tragic killings, and the consequences of this event are now reaching their fruition. The youngsters' innocent blood transformed the surrounding maize stalks into wahuapas, malevolent maizefolk who prey on the living. These sentient creatures are easily mistaken for ordinary plants, a trait they use to their maximum benefit while they steadily transform the wild grasses into a self-contained maze-like compound by manipulating the plants' growth into a shape and design of their own bizarre creation. Over the past year, the monsters have slowly expanded their range closer to the village where they have now begun to exact their vengeance on the villagers, claiming their first victim just the night before the adventure unfolds.

Heroes drawn into these events must first unmask a wahuapa (maizefolk) as the culprit behind the village's first killing and also untangle the other facets of this complex situation. In the year since Conto and Chipinia's untimely death, the young man's prospective bride Ciahuatl has not forgotten her betrothed. She made a pact with the cihuateteo, the malevolent spirits of women who died in childbirth, to give her the power to avenge his death, which she firmly believes came at the hands of another villager. Later that evening, the cacalotls she breathed to life also descend on the settlement, requiring the characters to intervene to save innocent lives. Meanwhile, Uetzopilli's reanimated corpse actively seeks out his killers, though the undead monstrosity stops at nothing in his quest to exact his brutal brand of frontier justice. After resolving these simultaneous machinations and while gathering more clues in the process, the characters come to the conclusion that the tragic events now plaguing Pilhua all stem from the murders that took place more than one year earlier.

With this knowledge in hand, the characters trek out into the substantially altered maizefield where Conto and Chipinia met their tragic end. The unrequited siblings manipulated the landscape to create a seemingly impossible structure of twisted vegetation and hardened cornstalks that form a contorted maze. The heroes must navigate their way through this treacherous complex of deadly traps, hideous guardians, and grisly sights until they arrive at the makeshift gravesite where the children's remarkably well-preserved bodies still lie. The formerly innocent souls are now malevolent spirits who loathe the living and endeavor to spread their blight into the neighboring village and ultimately across the land unless the characters can stop them and hopefully administer some justice of their own to the callous murderers who caused their untimely deaths.

ADVENTURE SUMMARY

This adventure has several moving parts that may make it appear daunting to run at first glance. It includes red herrings and some investigative digging to unlock the mystery, which will likely consume several hours of gameplay as the characters sort through the evidence and testimony to reach their

AREA MAP
N
Maizefield
*
Village
Square
Noble Houses
1 Square – 500 Feet

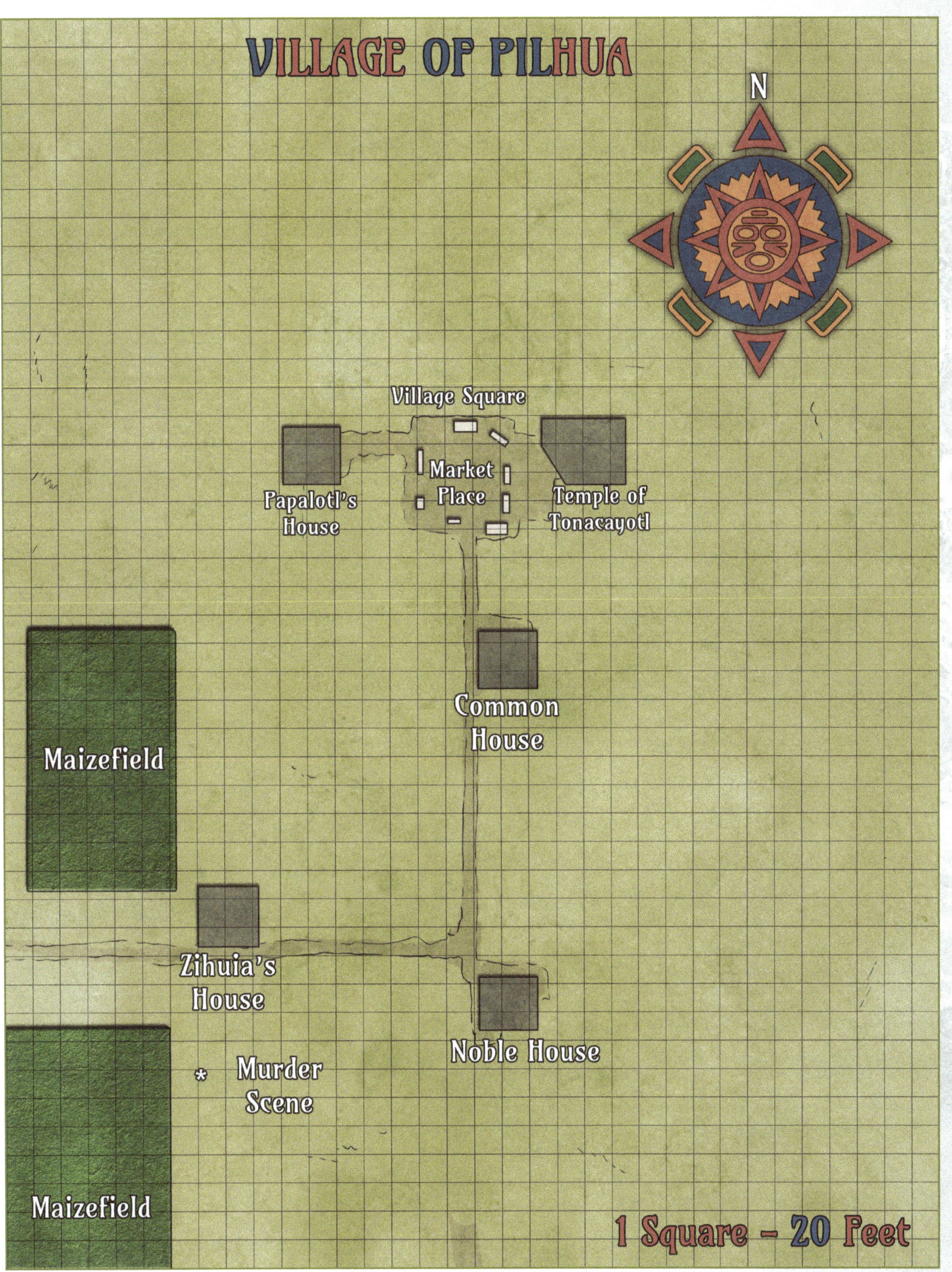

VILLAGE OF PILHUA
N
Village Square
Papalotl's House
Market Place
Temple of Tonacayotl
Maizefield
Common House
Zihuia's House
* Murder Scene
Noble House
Maizefield
1 Square - 20 Feet

conclusions. Two forthcoming sections, **Places of Interest** and **People of Interest**, detail the information the adventurers can gather from those sites and individuals. To avoid confusion and to keep the adventure on track, these are the key facts in the story:

• A wahuapa (maizefolk) camouflaged itself as an ordinary maize plant in Zihuia's field and waited for an opportunity to attack and kill a random victim (Zihuia) to sow terror in the village. After the killing, the creature fled back to the manipulated maizefield outside the village.

• Zihuia and Icihua's marital and financial difficulties are just red herrings. They play no role in the murder.

• Ciahuatl, Conto's fiancée, blames the town's leader, Papalotl, for failing to find her betrothed, prompting her to direct her cacalotls to attack Papalotl and the villagers.

• Mixoch and Temilaz's other victim, Uetzopilli, emerged from the grave as a sword wight who makes his way to Pilhua to seek revenge against his murderers.

• The wahuapas plan to return to the village to take more innocent lives unless the characters stop them.

The trail of death and mayhem ultimately leads back to Conto and Chipinia's killing more than one year ago where the two unrequited horrors created an enclosed maze crafted from manipulated maize plants.

STARTING THE ADVENTURE

The characters are free to start the adventure in the village of Pilhua or while traveling through the area on their way somewhere else. Ideally the characters arrive sometime during the day or the early evening because the story's events unfold rather quickly over the course of the first evening and throughout the overnight hours. An earlier arrival allows the adventurers an opportunity to get the lay of the land and to become embroiled in the mystery gripping Pilhua rather than trying to catch up on details after the fact. Of course, if the characters make their way to the village very late in the evening, you can delay the adventure's events until the following evening and allow the characters to explore the village and gather some information before getting the tale fully underway. In every case, the adventure's opening act generally starts with the characters hearing about Zihuia's mysterious killing and investigating it.

Although the adventure is intended to be set on the island of Tehuatl, which is a new addition to the world of the Lost Lands, you can have the adventure take place in any village of your choosing with some minor adjustments.

ADVENTURE HOOKS

You may use any of the following devices to get the characters involved in the storyline shortly before or when they arrive in Pilhua.

JUSTICE NEVER DONE

It has been more than one year since their children Conto and Chipinia disappeared from their home one day and never returned. Despite an exhaustive search and the village's sympathy, the teenagers' parents, **Itoloc** and **Namaquia**, remain determined to find their missing son and daughter. They are resolute that something untoward happened to them, but they cannot offer any evidence supporting their assertion or further leads regarding their whereabouts. When they learned about Zihuia's murder, they believe his death must have some correlation to their children's predicament as killings are extremely rare in the settlement. While gnolls and other monsters have troubled the village throughout its history, they always leave telltale hallmarks of their presence whenever they strike. Itoloc and Namaquia cannot offer any monetary reward, but they happily arrange a marriage with their surviving son **Oquimon** or priestess daughter **Nequilti** to a character who returns their children to them or discovers their true fate. See the upcoming **Speaking with the Family** sidebar for more details about the information they can provide to the characters during their interactions with them.

MURDER MOST FOUL

Zihuia's widow, **Icihua**, has little confidence in the local authorities solving her deceased husband's murder. Icihua descends from Itztliteotl, making her one of the village's few coconeteotls (nobles) and giving her greater pull and status within Pilhua than the children's commoner parents. Despite her overt melancholy and hysteria, some wary villagers cast a suspicious eye toward the grieving widow who openly flirted with younger warriors throughout her marriage to Zihuia, who was also a nobleperson of lesser rank than his spouse. Cognizant of these chattering voices, the wealthy woman approaches the characters to investigate the matter and ultimately clear her name. Of course, she denies any involvement in his death, which is a truthful assertion, though she gets more squirrelly when asked about her professed love for her husband and the rumors about her affairs with other men. While in her late 30s, the childless Icihua remains a charming, attractive woman with considerable financial means compared to her fellow villagers. She offers the characters a personal family heirloom and a pair of turquoise earplugs worth 250 gp to primarily absolve her of any involvement in the killing, and secondarily to solve the case. If you use this hook, see the upcoming **Speaking with Icihua** sidebar for details regarding Icihua's knowledge about the crime.

AN EXPLOSIVE SITUATION

Not all maize is created equally nor serves the same purpose. The small village of Pilhua is like many others scattered across the Caya Grasslands, but some inhabitants swear the farmers who live here grow the finest popcorn on the island and season the exploding kernels better than anyone else. Maize aficionados consider the pilgrimage to the community to be worth the effort. If you opt to use this hook, the characters themselves may be on their way to the town to partake in a popcorn festival that occurs during the 10th day of every month, or they are traveling here at the behest of someone else who sent them to purchase two bushels of popcorn from a local pochteca. In this case, the characters may visit the murderers Mixoch and Temilaz to conduct the legitimate transactions (see the **Speaking with Mixoch and Temilaz** sidebar). During their stay in the village, the characters ultimately learn about the killing and may be prompted to further explore the matter of their own accord or at another party's request.

PART ONE: THE VILLAGE OF PILHUA

With a population just under 300 residents, the predominately Aztli community of Pilhua is an agrarian community where its resident farmers cultivate maize along with squash, quinoa, tomatoes, chili peppers, and cilantro. The town's 271 commoners live on land they lease at a low cost from the town's 26 nobles including its seven coconeteotls and Icihua, the widow of the murder victim Zihuia who was also a noble of lesser status than his spouse. Pilhua stretches out across roughly two square miles of ground with the nobility living in furnished, multiroom homes clustered around the village's aqueducts that divert water into the community from neighboring rivers and streams, while the commoners occupy simple one-room abodes built on chinampas along Pilhua's outskirts and edges. Regardless of social status, each residence also features an attached temazcal that functions as a primitive sauna where family members can relax and also cleanse their bodies after an arduous day in the fields.

When not at home or tending to their crops, villagers gather on the grounds of the Temple of Tonacayotl where vibrant stalks of the vital plant tower almost 10 feet above the earth. Here, they exchange the news of the day while socializing with their neighbors as well as bringing offerings of maize to the deity venerated within this humble yet important religious center. **Cintecuhtli** tends to his worshippers' spiritual and earthly needs. A fellow coconeteotl in his own right, Cintecuhtli is an influential village member, though his authority rarely extends beyond matters outside his sacred purview. Instead, **Papalotl** exercises secular authority over the village. He and his contingent of **17 jaguar warriors** keep the peace within Pilhua. Papalotl is a quichtic, a noble title earned through his bravery on the battlefield that he earned in his youth when he singlehandedly felled seven gnolls during a raid more than 30 years ago. Now approaching 50 years of age, Papalotl frequently relives the glory days of his younger days when his fighting skills were at their zenith.

Cintecuhtli, Male Aztli Human Priest of Tonacayotl (Clr4):
HP 19; **AC** 5[14]; **Atk** club (1d6); **Move** 12; **Save** 12; **AL** N; **CL/XP** 5/240; **Special:** +2 save vs. paralyzation and poison, banish undead, spells (2/1).
Spells: 1st—*cure light wounds, purify food and drink*; 2nd—*bless*.
Equipment: olli armor[B], club.

Jaguar Warriors, Male or Female Aztli Humans (17):
HD 1; **AC** 8[11]; **Atk** itztopillis (1d6); **Move** 12; **Save** 17; **AL** Any; **CL/XP** 1/15; **Special:** none. (***Monstrosities*** 257)
Equipment: ichcahuipilli armor[B], itztopilli[B].

Papalotl, Male Aztli Human (Ftr4): HP 28; **AC** 4[15]; **Atk** macuahuitl (1d8); **Move** 12; **Save** 14; **AL** N; **CL/XP** 4/120; **Special:** multiple attacks (4) vs. creatures with 1 or fewer HD.
Equipment: ollixalli armor[B], macuahuitl[B].
[B] See **Appendix B: New Items and Magic**

Most families' roots in the village go back multiple generations with many residents being at least distantly related to each other. The human Aztlis dominate the community, with a handful of half-elf Poqozas and elves from the neighboring forest as well as several halflings rounding out the settlement. Self-sufficient farming accounts for a substantial percentage of Pilhua's economy, with some families selling surplus yields to visiting merchants outside the Temple of Tonacayotl. However, there are 23 artisans of different races in the village who manufacture goods such as leather, adventuring gear and equipment, tools, implements, herbal remedies, artworks, and other specialty items catering to villagers and the officially licensed pochtecas who frequent the crude marketplace outside the holy site's vestibule.

RUMORS

Outside of a tiny minority of newcomers in Pilhua, everyone generally knows everyone else in the community for nearly their entire lives. The close bonds ensure that information, for better or worse, travels fast across the village, though accuracy sometimes takes a back seat to the news' hasty delivery. While exploring the settlement, the characters may overhear information from locals or actively gather it. Roll d20 once on the table below. Give the characters all the information with a target number equal to or lower than the number rolled.

TABLE 1-1: RUMORS

d20	Rumor
3	The Temple of Tonacayotl is the only religious building in the village and the hub of activity in Pilhua. Most people gather here to discuss news, sell their crops, and socialize when not working in the fields. (This rumor is true.)
4	Cintecuhtli, the high priest of Tonacayotl, is a good, honest man. Many villagers revere him as a father figure. He attends to all spiritual ceremonies and rites in the settlement. (This rumor is true.)
5	Someone murdered a local man named Zihuia. Everyone except the authorities suspect that his wife Icihua knows more than she is saying about the killing. (This rumor is true.)
6	Pilhua is under the Aztli Confederation's jurisdiction, and Papalotl serves as the village's foremost secular authority. (This rumor is true.)
7	If you need any goods, Mixoch and Temilaz, the local pochtecas, are the men to see. (This rumor is true.)
8	The gnolls have been more active lately. An attack is imminent. (This rumor is false.)
9-10	Poqoza traders sometimes visit Pilhua to peddle illegal substances such as intoxicating mushrooms and cacti. (This rumor is partly true since Uetzopilli no longer comes here.)
11-12	Two local siblings, Conto and Chipinia, vanished from the village roughly one year ago. An exhaustive search of the village and the surrounding area turned up no traces of the teenagers or their ultimate fate. (This rumor is true.)
13	Conto was engaged to Ciahuatl. She is bitter about the lack of progress in finding her fiancé and has grown distant and melancholy since his disappearance. (This rumor is true.)
14-15	Zihuia and Icihua had numerous problems during their marriage. Zihuia drank too much and dabbled in drugs. She is too flirtatious and has supposedly had affairs with others, though no one has ever admitted to that. (This rumor is true.)
16	Mixoch and Temilaz supply psychedelic substances on occasion, though they have not done so ever since Cintecuhtli spoke to them about the dangers and morality of doing so. (This rumor is partly true, as the pair stopped selling drugs but not because of the high priest's interference.)
17-18	A priest of the gnoll's god Itzcuin has infiltrated the village and is distracting the residents to pave the way for an attack. (This rumor is false.)

d20	Rumor
19	Spilt innocent blood can give birth to the dreaded wahuapa, the maizefolk who occasionally stalk the grasslands. These sentient plants hate all humanoid life and seek to destroy it. (This rumor is true.)
20	When a teenager dies tragically, the soul may be reborn as an undead spirit approximately one year after their death. (This rumor describes how the unrequited form and is true.)

The last two rumors describe two of the monsters found in the adventure. If you don't want the characters to receive them as random rumors, you could instead require a character to make a specific inquiry or conduct appropriate research about each topic to learn them.

POINTS OF INTEREST

The following section details important points of interest the characters find within Pilhua. The characters are free to explore the village in its entirety, though most homes and their adjoining land provide nothing of interest to solving the mystery enveloping the community.

TEMPLE OF TONACAYOTL

Although primarily designed to be a religious center, the single-story Temple of Tonacayotl proves to be multifunctional. The mud-brick structure includes an outer vestibule where worshippers and villagers gather, and an inner shrine where followers offer maize at the feet of a limestone man-sized statue of the god depicted as a young man with yellow hair. The god of maize is the sculpture's divine subject. Smaller religious iconography dedicated to the other members of the Aztli pantheon occupy small niches built into the circular chamber's walls. These include paintings and miniature wood figurines of Yaocteotl, Itztliteotl, Zipe-Toteque, Quiahuitl, Nonotzali, and Micoateotl. While the Aztlis still provide offerings to these deities, Tonacayotl's priest Cintecuhtli performs no formal rites or ceremonies to honor them. Nonetheless, Pilhua's Aztli residents still venerate these important gods and honor them in the sanctity of their homes.

Cintecuhtli also resides within the temple, dwelling in a bland room connected to the inner shrine that contains a plain, linen mat for sleeping and a small enclosed alcove for steam bathing. The middle-aged priest never married and devoted his life to praising Tonacayotl, who has blessed the village with bountiful crops throughout his 22-year tenure and serves as the village's de facto healer. Cintecuhtli uses medicinal herbs he grows in a garden on the temple grounds to remedy minor ailments and illnesses. For more serious injuries, the priest relies upon the magical powers his benefactor grants him to close wounds and to cure diseases. Despite living alone for nearly his entire adult life, Cintecuhtli is a gregarious man who enjoys the company of others. Despite holding the lesser noble title of tlahtoh for his services to the temple, the village priest frequently dines at the homes of commoners who welcome him into their humble abodes with open arms. He is renowned for his ability

ZIHUIA'S CORPSE

Still clothed in his bloody cloak, the body displays eight laceration wounds across his body: one on his face, two on his back, two on his right arm, two on his right leg, and a final slice across his abdomen. A sharp, serrated weapon or appendage inflicted the injuries. A character who closely examines the body has a 2-in-6 chance to find tiny strands of greenish-brown, silky fibers embedded in the wounds. These are fibers from a maize husk, which seems inexplicable as Zihuia was not found in the maizefield and had no contact with the plants. Cintecuhtli has no explanation for how the corn silk got into the wounds, as he cleaned the body with a cloth.

If the characters communicate with Zihuia's spirit through a *speak with the dead* spell or similar magic, the victim communicates only what he saw. Because of his severely intoxicated state at the time of his killing, his answers are basic and vague. He recalls feeling a sharp object tear through his skin several times and makes a cryptic reference to the "damn maize stalk wrapping around him."

to shape perfectly round tortillas and his ability to flawlessly season any maize dish, which runs counter to his vanilla lifestyle choices. Because of his extensive contacts with the villagers, he is practically the fountain of all information in Pilhua.

Zihuia's recent murder greatly disturbs him. Naturally, he turned to Tonacayotl for magical guidance and received a cryptic response telling him "the sins of the present have deep roots in the past." He also cleansed Zihuia's body before its cremation, which he plans to attend to the following morning. The temple stores the corpse in a cellar underneath the inner shrine that is accessible through a door in the floor. If the characters ask to see the body, Cintecuhtli politely declines their request. However, persuasive characters can overcome his initial reluctance and be granted permission to examine Zihuia's lifeless body, though Cinteciuhtli still insists on maintaining proper decorum while doing so.

During any discussion about the killing, Cintecuhtli makes an offhanded remark about Conto and Chipinia. He nonchalantly tells the characters that his followers never experienced these types of crimes for most of his time here, but first it was the missing children and now a murdered villager. If the characters probe for more details, Cintecuhtli vividly recalls praying with the family and conducting extensive searches throughout the area looking for the lost siblings with no luck. He presumes they either ran away, which he highly doubts, or met a tragic end, likely at the hands of gnolls who occasionally raid outlying farms. He laments that the family still hopes to find their precious son and daughter, but he sadly believes their efforts to be in vain. He also mentions that Conto's fiancée Ciahuatl still grieves for the man she was to marry and has withdrawn into her own melancholy.

When he returns to the subject of Zihuia's death, he also expresses frustration and uncertainty. If asked for a connection between the man's killing and the children's disappearance, none readily comes to mind. The nobleman had little if any contact with the young commoners. If asked about Icihua, the grieving widow, he does not believe that she had any role in her husband's killing. Nonetheless, he reluctantly relents that her flirtatiousness could lead some to speculate that she played a part in his death. However, Cintecuhtli also admits that Zihuia had plenty of flaws, including a penchant for drinking too much pulque and occasionally embarking on mind trips using psychedelics smuggled into the village from south of the Great Canal. If the characters ask him about the latter topic, he says that Zihuia had not partaken in this indulgence for at least several months, though characters who roll below their wisdom on 3d6 believe that there is more to the story than he initially acknowledges. If the characters press him further about the matter, he reluctantly admits that Mixoch and Temilaz, two local pochtecas, supposedly sold psychedelic mushrooms and other hallucinogens they acquired from Poqoza traders, but they seem to no longer be involved in selling these goods in the village, a fact he attributes to a conversation he had with the pair several months earlier in response to Zihuia's erratic behavior.

Finding Mixoch and Temilaz (see the **Mixoch** and **Temilaz** section) proves easy during the day. The temple grounds serve as a meeting place for villagers and the center of commerce within the community, and the two pochtecas conduct business here throughout the day alongside farmers, artisans, and other local residents peddling their goods. The duo hustles their wares to their regular customers who venture to the temple grounds only once per week or every other week.

Venlo Innova is also a mainstay in the public marketplace. The halfling inventor fashions himself as an "improver" rather than an innovator. He enhances already existing items with mixed success. Venlo lives and works out of his shop roughly one-half mile from the temple. He lugs his goods back and forth with him using a modified sled that he drags along the ground on his way to and from his home, which offers an example of one of his more productive design upgrades. Venlo also imagines himself to be an amateur investigator who once again demonstrates uneven performance. He excels at analyzing and interpreting physical evidence, yet he fails miserably at gathering testimony and interacting with others. He is prone to making outlandish accusations, even though the facts he uncovered refute his assertions, and he baselessly thinks everyone lies to him. Venlo's shortcomings aside, the halfling gladly offers to sell his adventuring gear to prospective customers as well as offer his opinions and assistance if the characters ask questions about Zihuia's killing or the missing children.

Venlo Innova, Male Halfling (MU3): HP 9; AC 8[11] or 2[17] (missile) and 4[15] (melee) from *shield* spell; **Atk** staff (1d6) or darts x3 (1d3); **Move** 12; **Save** 12 (+1, ring); **AL** C; **CL/XP** 3/60; **Special:** +1 missile weapon bonus, +2 save vs. spells, wands and staffs, spells, +4 save vs. magic, spells (3/1).
Spells: 1st—*detect magic, magic missile, shield*; 2nd—*phantasmal force*.
Equipment: staff, 6 darts, *ring of protection +1*.

Venlo the Detective

The characters are free to use Venlo's services at their peril. Venlo theorizes Conto and Chipinia were abducted by astral travelers he believes came from one of the planet's two moons. His "proof" for this theory derives from the villagers' inability to find any physical evidence regarding their fate. He thinks only supernatural beings could accomplish such a feat. Fortunately, he has not yet formulated a solid theory about Zihuia's death, though he leans toward exploring crackpot explanations over rational ones, including the return of his imaginary astral travelers, Zihuia's supposed involvement with an agricultural cabal intent on replacing maize with amaranth, and assassins who masquerade as mice. However, if the characters inspect the murder scene and perform certain other tasks with Venlo in tow, he can provide another set of eyes and ears to examine the facts of the case while trying to steer him away from the fantastical.

Zihuia's Home (The Murder Scene)

Although members of nobility, the home Zihuia shared with his wife **Icihua** seems hardly fitting for one of the village's best-known power couples. It is modestly sized even when compared to the commoners' residences, and it has hardly any amenities for people of their status. The surprisingly rundown abode's only selling point is its location. A character who visits the site takes note of the unkempt property's poor condition for people of such purported means.

Icihua found her husband's body facedown at the edge of their small farm roughly 110 feet from the door shortly before midnight. A character who searches the area discovers pottery shards littering the ground between the residence and the murder location. A character who examines the pieces can identify the shards as part of a jar that contained pulque. However, Papalotl removed the corpse shortly after arriving on the scene. When the characters arrive here, the only evidence they find are three streaks of blood covering the soil 15 feet from the first row of maize flourishing in the fertile earth.

The plants appear ordinary from a distance. However, a character who enters into the maizefield and walks among the stalks notices a deep hole in the ground approximately 45 feet from the murder scene. The disturbed earth is loose yet still moist. A character who examines the dirt concludes the ground was excavated within the last 24 hours. Furthermore, the abscess oddly appears in a spot between two rows of maize, indicating that no one planted maize in the unearthed location. Further digging in the cavity reveals no residual roots or other fibrous plant material around the hole's edges. A character has a 1-in-6 chance to locate an unusual set of tracks leading from the void toward the murder scene (3-in-6 chance for rangers and druids). The visible depressions in the ground appear to be made by something fibrous or tendril-like rather than humanoid or even monstrous feet. The character surmises that some type of vine or other plant material made the impressions in the ground. While it is possible to follow the trail from the hole to the murder site, Papalotl and his warriors made footprints around where the blood splattered, making it impossible to distinguish where the presumed perpetrator went afterward.

Common House

The villagers use this lodge to accommodate visitors, though its furnishings are sparse and amenities limited. It is simply an open space with linen mats for sleeping and a steam room for bathing. If the characters opt to stay here during their visit to Pilhua, there is no cost, though it is customary to make an offering to the Temple of Tonacayotl for its hospitality in maintaining and cleaning the facility. Guests are also expected to keep the common house tidy and exhibit proper etiquette while staying in the equivalent of someone else's home. Although there are no other visitors at the time, farmhands and nobles occasionally wander in to gather some news about the world outside of Pilhua.

People of Interest

The preceding section describes the characters' interactions with Cintecuhtli, the high priest of Tonacayotl, Venlo Innova the halfling inventor, and Icihua, the grieving widow. However, the characters are likely to want to speak with

Speaking with Icihua

Characters who venture to Zihuia's murder site are likely to eventually meet with and speak to his widow, Icihua. Rumors constantly swirl around the noblewoman, yet contrary to these stories, she never betrayed Zihuia even though she had ample reason to do so on many occasions. If the adventurers speak to her, the vivacious woman falls back on her natural instinct to charm her attentive audience. Icihua's account of the events leading up to the murder are truthful, though she may gloss over an inconvenient fact when it suits her needs. She provides the following information without coaxing:

• Around midnight, she and Zihuia got into an argument over his excessive pulque consumption. Her husband stormed out of their home with a jar of pulque in hand.

• When he did not return within a few minutes like he usually would, she left the home to look for him. In the moonlight, she saw him lying face down on the ground. Naturally, she presumed he had passed out again, but when she drew closer to check on him, she noticed that blood had soaked his cloak.

• Gashes tore through the fabric and his flesh. She could tell he had stopped breathing and was obviously dead. Fearful that whatever harmed her husband might still be out there, she rushed to summon Papalotl for aid and to investigate the crime.

• Although he clearly died a violent death, Icihua heard nothing after Zihuia left and before she discovered the body.

• She and her husband own the land, which they lease to multiple commoner families who live on the village's outskirts. They collect a percentage of their crop yields, which they use to feed themselves and also to sell for additional income. To the best of her knowledge, no one has been in the maizefield for several days because of the persistent rain.

Icihua readily volunteers the preceding information, but she intentionally withholds the following details from the characters. Engaging in one of the following lines of questioning requires the character to already possess some facts pertaining to the subject matter.

Financial Problems: Icihua acknowledges that her husband squandered his money on pulque, hallucinogens, and fly-by-night schemes. A few times, he came close to risking his noble status because of his misfortune, but they always paid his creditors in the end.

Drug Use: Icihua admits Zihuia used psychedelic substances on some occasions, but says he had not done so for at least the past several months. If pressed about where he obtained the hallucinogens, she believes Mixoch and Temilaz sold them to him, but he never specifically told her where he purchased them.

Maizefield Hole: Icihua knows nothing about the anomalous hole in the maizefield. She swears they planted their seeds in perfect rows. She never saw any strange activity there.

Her Indiscretions: Icihua vehemently denies any allegations about her infidelity. She begrudgingly confesses to sometimes being too flirtatious toward her male and even female admirers, though her relationships never went beyond friendship or playful banter.

Possible Suspects: She swears no one had any reason to harm her husband. He had settled his debts and no longer partook in drug use. Excessive pulque consumption was his worst problem, and no one would kill him over drinking too much.

other individuals in town while conducting their investigation. The following paragraphs describe their interactions with other residents who can shed some light on the events plaguing Pilhua as well as some directly responsible for setting the tragic chain of events into motion.

Conto and Chipinia's Family

Characters who learn of the siblings' disappearance one year earlier may wish to speak with their family to learn more about the teenagers and to get some additional insight from them about their suspected fate. If you used the **Justice Never Done** hook, the characters may acquire this information from the family members at the adventure's onset. The children's father **Itoloc** and mother **Namaquia** still mourn the presumed loss of their middle son and daughter. Their older son **Omiquin** and younger daughter **Nequilti** also suffer on a daily basis though they are more resilient than their aging and obviously

Speaking with the Family

Itoloc and Namaquia readily volunteer everything they know about that fateful day without coaxing.

• Conto and Chipinia were extremely close and frequently traveled together throughout the village and sometimes beyond it. Nonetheless, they always came home safe afterward.

• No one recalls seeing them that day, which is unusual because they knew everyone and would frequently encounter someone during the course of their travels.

• They never said where they were going that day.

• Conto never would have left of his own accord. He deeply loved his fiancée Ciahuatl and looked forward to marrying her in the coming days.

• Gnolls have periodically attacked the village or raided outlying farms, but there were no other reports of their activity in the days before or following their disappearance.

Nequilti and her sister, who was 16 months older, did not have the same tight bond as her two older siblings. However, the pair sometimes confided in their older brother Omiquin. Despite his concern for his missing siblings, he is a little more tightlipped than his parents. He is not as forthright as everyone else when discussing the matter with the rest of the family. If characters press him for further details, Omiquin asks the character to step outside his parents' earshot to convey his additional information:

• His younger brother and sister liked to smoke tobacco and drink pulque that he acquired for them on occasion. They frequently went to one of several isolated areas outside village, but he showed Papalotl the places he knew about, and they found nothing.

• For a short while, the trio partook in ingesting peyote and psychedelic mushrooms. Omiquin stopped using them shortly after his siblings' disappearance.

• Ciahuatl took his brother's death very hard. She rarely if ever speaks to anyone unless forced to do so and endlessly obsesses over tragedies.

If the characters further question him about the narcotic substance use, they may be able to pry the final piece of information from the protective oldest brother:

• Omiquin purchased the substances from Mixoch and Temilaz, whom he believed acquired them from a pochteca trader. However, they stopped selling the illicit goods roughly one year ago. They never gave an explanation as to why other than vague hints about having a problem with their supplier.

• Although Omiquin primarily interacted with the pochtecas, his younger brother and sister were at least slightly familiar with them.

devastated parents. The family gladly welcomes anyone willing to uncover what really happened to their missing children.

Itoloc, Male Aztli Human: HP 6; AC 9[10]; **Atk** club (1d6); **Move** 12; **Save** 18; **AL** N; **CL/XP** B/10; **Special:** none. (*Monstrosities* 254)

Namaquia, Female Aztli Human: HP 2; AC 9[10]; **Atk** none; **Move** 12; **Save** 18; **AL** N; **CL/XP** B/10; **Special:** none. (*Monstrosities* 254)

Nequilti, Female Aztli Human: HP 3; AC 9[10]; **Atk** dagger (1d6); **Move** 12; **Save** 18; **AL** N; **CL/XP** B/10; **Special:** none. (*Monstrosities* 254)

Omiquin, Male Aztli Human (Ftr2): HP 12; AC 8[11]; **Atk** macuahuitl (1d8); **Move** 12; **Save** 13; **AL** L; **CL/XP** 2/30; **Special:** multiple attacks (2) vs. creatures with 1 or fewer HD. **Equipment:** ichcahuipilli armor[B], macuahuitl[B].
[B] See **Appendix B: New Items and Magic**

Speaking with the Farmhands

Although not intentionally evasive, Nitla and Alihui are reluctant to speak ill of the nobles who own the land they lease. However, when questioned about the following subjects, they provide these answers without coaxing:

• *Zihuia/Icihua:* They and their family have worked for the couple since shortly after they married and acquired the land. The couple has problems from time to time, but so does everyone else.

• *Hole/Abscess:* The farmhands swear every row of maize was planted in straight lines. No one recalls ever seeing a cavity in the ground on the property or can explain how it got there.

The couple are more reluctant to discuss the following details, but they can be prodded into providing this information:

• *Zihuia's Lifestyle:* Zihuia occasionally dabbled in taking hallucinogens, but his main issue was his excessive pulque consumption. He and Icihua frequently argued about his alcoholism. However, when he was sober, which was less often than when he was drunk, Zihuia was an industrious and kind person.

• *Icihua's Lifestyle:* Despite the stories circulating within the village and her vivacious personality, Icihua remained faithful to her husband throughout their marriage. She certainly tired of Zihuia's vices, but she loved him nonetheless.

• *Financial Issues:* Zihuia's debts almost got the better of them, but they almost wriggled their way out of a tight spot and satisfied their creditors in the end.

Farmhands

Characters who meet with Icihua may wish to speak with the men and women who plant, till, and harvest the crops from her maizefield. In all, 14 adults work on Icihua's land, but the junior farmhands defer all questions to the team's de facto leaders **Nitla** and **Alihui**. The husband and wife team have worked for Zihuia and Icihua for 15 years along with their younger siblings, children, and extended family. They live in a small home on the village's outskirts roughly one-half mile from Zihuia's home.

Nitla, Male Aztli Human: HP 5; AC 9[10]; **Atk** club (1d6); **Move** 12; **Save** 18; **AL** N; **CL/XP** B/10; **Special:** none. (*Monstrosities* 254)

Alihui, Female Aztli Human: HP 3; AC 9[10]; **Atk** dagger (1d4); **Move** 12; **Save** 18; **AL** N; **CL/XP** B/10; **Special:** none. (*Monstrosities* 254)

Papalotl

The noble warrior Papalotl interacts with the Aztli Confederation's delegation from Ixtla and also wields secular authority on the alliance's behalf over Pilhua, though he is not an official member or representative of Ixtla or the confederation. Papalotl earned his stripes and well-earned reputation on the battlefield during his skirmishes against gnoll raiders and the occasional monster that plagued the village. He prefers fighting an obvious enemy he can see and has little interest or talent for unraveling mysteries. When he arrived at the scene of the crime, Papalotl was more interested in tracking down the perpetrator through military means rather than gathering evidence and unmasking the culprit. Because he and his soldiers so badly trampled down the area around Zihuia's body, even the recent spate of rain could not preserve any tracks or trail leading away from the crime scene.

Papalotl becomes very defensive if the characters question his investigative skills or his actions. In that case, he terminates the conversation with them and refuses to answer any additional questions. If the characters persist, he ultimately threatens to arrest them and turn them over to the authorities in Ixtla for a stay in the peticalli (Aztli penitentiary). The warriors under his command cannot provide any additional information beyond what Papalotl already provided.

Speaking with Ciahuatl

Characters who meet Ciahuatl encounter an aloof, distant young woman obsessed with finding her missing lover and avenging him if something untoward happened to him. She speaks as little as possible and frequently makes facial expressions and gestures indicating her clear disinterest in helping the heroes. While her justifiable fury led her down a vile path, she is not wholly irredeemable. When portraying Ciahuatl during her meeting with the characters, it is important to remember that she is still not an adult and has never committed a truly evil act during her short lifetime. Her dejection and lack of trust in the abilities of others has basis in fact. Getting through her tough exterior and appealing to her remaining vestiges of humanity poses a significant challenge to the characters.

Getting her to say anything at all is difficult, but if characters do, she offers only the following vague details with a detached attitude:

• Conto and his younger sister disappeared a little more than one year ago.

• The villagers went looking for them, but could not find them. Then again, Papalotl and his soldiers could not find a jaguar in an empty room.

• She was deeply in love with Conto and was committed to spending the rest of her life with him and having a family.

• No one else will ever make her happy.

Getting any additional information beyond these cursory items proves exceptionally difficult as the haughty teenager ignores the strangers and declines to answer any more questions, claiming she has nothing further to say about the matter. She reverts to staring blankly into space and softly singing lullabies to assuage her anguish and to reinforce her unwillingness to continue the conversation with the characters. Bullying, belittling, or lying to her are ineffective tactics and only further her resolve not to cooperate. If the characters resort to these methods, she grows tired of their presence and demands that they leave her sight at once.

Characters who refuse are in for a rude awakening as the clever Ciahuatl escorts the characters out of her home and discreetly signals for the **8 cacalotls** hiding in the maizefield outside her home to attack the characters after they leave the residence. The monsters behave as described in the **Murder of Cacalotls** section, though in this instance, Ciahuatl stays out of the fray, leaving the constructs to fend for themselves while feigning having no pre-existing relationship with the monsters. If the characters leave of their own accord, the cacalotls remain silent and continue to hide in the field.

Cacalotls (8): HD 4; **HP** 28, 25, 24, 21, 19x2, 17, 16; **AC** 9[10]; **Atk** 2 claws (1d6 + poison); **Move** 12; **Save** 13; **AL** C; **CL/XP** 5/240; **Special:** camouflage (when motionless, appears as ordinary doll or scarecrow), cackle (1/day, 30ft radius, save or 2d6 damage and frightened as *fear* spell, save for half damage and avoids fear), darkvision (60ft), poison (save or additional 1d4 damage), vulnerable to fire (200% damage). (see **Appendix A: New Monsters**)

If a character identifies Mixoch and Temilaz as her fiancé's killer and can offer at least a scintilla of proof, characters can break through Ciahuatl's tough exterior. The young woman is not irreparably evil, at least not yet, and can be swayed from her current course of action with the proper coaxing. In this case, Ciahuatl breaks down and tells the characters the following information:

• She suspects someone murdered Conto and Chipinia and that their deaths played a central role in the formation of an enclosed maizefield outside the village. The exact link eludes her, but she knows the wahuapas (maizefolk) guard the entrance to the complex.

• Spilt humanoid blood creates wahuapas, and at least one of these creatures is responsible for killing Zihuia. She believes the monsters started hunting her down after she traveled to the manipulated maizefield several days earlier.

• Conto's older brother Omiquin sometimes gave his younger brother and sister pulque, tobacco, and occasionally other hallucinogens that he acquired from an unknown source. The pair would occasionally ingest and smoke in secluded locales outside the village.

Papalotl has no love for words or speaking with others, but if the characters interview him about the murder or the children's disappearance, the gruff soldier first asks about their authority to pose such questions to him. However, Papalotl is not the sharpest macuahuitl in the army. If characters get him talking, Papalotl reveals the following details about the evening of Zihuia's murder:

• Icihua summoned Papalotl and his troops to her home after discovering Zihuia's body outside their home several minutes earlier. When he and his subordinates examined the body, they noticed lacerations that tore through his clothing and sliced through his skin, killing him.

• He and his soldiers fanned out throughout the area but could find no physical evidence that would lead to a potential suspect or a trail.

• Everyone knew Zihuia and Icihua had issues, but he understood they were working through their issues. Icihua told him that Zihuia left the house after an argument and that she heard nothing until she found his body. Zihuia appeared genuinely shocked and saddened by her husband's untimely demise.

• He and his soldiers took Zihuia's body to the Temple of Tonacayotl for funerary rights.

CIAHUATL

Conto's grieving fiancée may be only 16 years of age, but her youth cannot comfort her pain. She deeply mourns the loss of her prospective future husband. The melancholy teenager also seethes that she and his family never received justice. **Ciahuatl** expresses her sorrow and anger by refusing to wash her face, wear jewelry, or tend to her luxurious hair, which has grown tangled and unmanageable. She eats just enough to survive and spends nearly all her time in a secluded enclave several hundred feet beyond her family's maizefield communing with the cihuateteo. Her parents **Otla** (N male Aztli human **commoner**) and **Coyani** (LN female Aztli human **commoner**) are at a loss to help their distraught daughter rebuild her shattered life.

The aloof young woman blames Papalotl's ineptitude and the villagers' lack of determination and ingenuity for failing to locate Conto and his missing sister. In her darkest hours, she struck a bargain with the cihuateteo to grant her the power to succeed where all others have failed. During her travels, she located the manipulated maizefield outside the village, though she could not get past the wahuapas guarding it to further investigate the site. She believes it holds the secret to unraveling the mystery of Conto and Chipinia's fate, but the wahuapas' attack last night convinced her that they are searching for her, which forced her to spring into action earlier than she hoped as described in the **Murder of Cacalotls** section.

Ciahuatl, Female Aztli Human: HD 8; HP 28; AC 9[10] or 2[17] (missile) and 4[15] (melee) from *shield* spell; **Atk** tecpatl (1d6); **Move** 12; **Save** 8; **AL** N (but becoming C); **CL/XP** 9/1100; **Special:** baleful melancholy (3/day, 30ft radius, target must save or suffer −1 penalty to hit, saves, and armor class for 1 hour), crushing despair (1/day, 30ft radius, save or 2d6 damage from crushing despair, save for half), darkvision (60ft), immune to charm and fear, spells (4/3/3/2 MU), twisted thoughts (anyone reading her mind must save or become frightened as *fear* spell) **Spells:** 1st—*charm person, magic missile, shield, sleep*; 2nd—*darkness 15ft radius, invisibility, mirror image*; 3rd—*hold person, lightning bolt, suggestion*; 4th—*confusion, fear*. **Equipment:** tecpatl[B].
[B] see **Appendix B: New Items and Magic**

If the characters win over Ciahuatl, she agrees to lead them to the maizefield complex and help them infiltrate it, though that is as far as she goes under that circumstance. On the other hand, characters who antagonize or fail to garner her support suffer her full wrath as described in the **Murder of Cacalotls** section. Ciahuatl's personal treasure is also described under that section.

The gregarious pochtecas converse at breakneck speed reminiscent of a carnival barker or auctioneer trying to close a deal or drive up the price of a worthless item. Despite their rapid-fire approach, the two keep a wary eye and ear open for potentially problematic subjects and poseurs trying to pry information out of them under the guise of partaking in a business transaction. Their experience and guile have kept them alive and out of the peticalli throughout their 40 years in this world. Zihuia's recent murder heightened their defenses as they expect someone to accuse them of the killing. They suspect someone may link them to occasionally providing psychedelic drugs to Zihuia and try to pin the murder on them because of their illicit business dealings. Throughout their conversation with the characters, Mixoch and Temilaz keep their guard up, and attempt to determine if the heroes are lying to them and to gauge their true motives for meeting with them. If the conversation steers toward topics they would prefer not to discuss, such as their dealings with Zihuia and the children's disappearance, they smugly stop talking and tell the busybodies to get lost.

Under no circumstances do they confess to killing Conto, Chipinia, or Uetzopilli unless magically compelled to do so. They deflect any questions about partaking in robberies or burglaries in other areas by citing that they cannot stop people from fabricating these stories. Yet they never specifically address the allegations by deflecting these questions with curt responses. They never willingly volunteer information to the characters:

Zihuia: They admit selling him psychedelic mushrooms and other hallucinogens on occasion, but have had no interactions with him for at least six months. He paid them in full for their products.

Omiquin: The pair claim Conto and Chipinia's older brother frequently sought them out for hallucinogenic herbs, tobacco, and pulque, which they provided until they ran out of hallucinogens about nine months ago.

Conto/Chipinia: They carefully say they had no dealings with Omiquin's younger siblings, which is a truthful statement. However, the pochtecas soft-soap their knowledge of them by saying they vaguely recall seeing them from time to time.

Drugs/Uetzopilli: A pochteca trader would sporadically supply them with psychedelics and hallucinogens, but they have not seen him for quite some time. If questioned about Uetzopilli after his re-emergence as a sword wight, Mixoch clams up, but Temilaz appears distressed about his reappearance.

MIXOCH AND TEMILAZ

The local pochtecas have been in the community for six years and have earned a reputation for being hard negotiators who can acquire exotic and illicit goods from their sources across the island. They are in their early 40s and pass themselves off as sophisticated world travelers, wearing fancy clothing and speaking with a regal demeanor. **Mixoch** and **Temilaz** may be held in high esteem for their business acumen, but the content of their character leaves much to be desired. The pair occasionally robs travelers passing through areas outside of town and have been implicated in several burglaries outside of Pilhua. Rumors of their involvement in these activities cast a cloud of suspicion over the tightknit duo who are rarely separated. Their interactions with the unreliable Poqoza merchant Uetzopilli set the adventure's events into motion when Conto and Chipinia witnessed them murder Uetzopilli, which unfortunately was not the only killing they have committed during their lengthy entrepreneurial and criminal careers.

Mixoch and Temilaz spend the majority of their day selling their wares in the marketplace outside the previously described **Temple of Tonacayotl**. The grifters have no personal residence and usually spend their nights at the **Common House**, the homes of noblepersons who conduct business with them, or sometimes they set up a makeshift camp just a stone's throw from their crude stand. Always on the hunt for new customers or suppliers, the two pochtecas happily engage strangers who may be interested in either avenue of business.

Mixoch, Male Aztli Human Pochteca (Merchant) (Thf8): HP

26; **AC** 8[11]; **Atk** macuahuitl (1d8) or sling (1d4); **Move** 12;
Save 8; **AL** C; **CL/XP** 8/800; **Special:** +2 save bonus vs. traps
and magical devices, backstab (x3), read languages, thieving
skills.
Thieving Skills: Climb 92%, Tasks/Traps 50%, Hear 5 in 6,
Hide 55%, Silent 60%, Locks 55%.
Equipment: ichcahuipill armor[B], macuahuitl[B], sling, 10 sling
stones, bag containing seven *+1 sling stones, potion of animal
control*, leather pouch containing six pearls (100 gp each), 36 gp.

Temilaz, Male Aztli Human Pochteca (Merchant) (Thf7):
HP 22; **AC** 8[11]; **Atk** macuahuitl (1d8) or sling (1d4); **Move** 12;
Save 9; **AL** C; **CL/XP** 7/600; **Special:** +2 save bonus vs. traps
and magical devices, backstab (x3), read languages, thieving
skills.
Thieving Skills: Climb 91%, Tasks/Traps 45%, Hear 5 in 6,
Hide 40%, Silent 50%, Locks 40%.
Equipment: ichcahuipill armor[B], macuahuitl[B], sling, 10 sling
stones, pouch containing 68 gp.
[B] See **Appendix B: New Items and Magic**

Characters who resort to magical means to gain information from Mixoch
and Temilaz through spells and magical effects may learn of the pair's
involvement in the murders more than one year earlier and may also receive
vague references to the location where the killings took place or the motives
behind them. When faced with a direct accusation, the duo spring into action
to silence anyone asking about these matters. They fight as a team. If faced
with imminent defeat, Temilaz reluctantly surrenders while Mixoch fights
to the bitter end. Temilaz can be made to admit to their role in Conto and
Chipinia's deaths as well as Uetzopilli's demise. Temilaz steadfastly denies
any part in Zihuia's murder and has no knowledge about that tragic crime.

Part Two:
Evil Descends on Pilhua

After the characters spend the first portion of the adventure gathering information and conducting their investigation in Pilhua, events kick into overdrive as the cacalotls, sword wight, and wahuapas all descend upon the village in rapid succession. Different leaders and motives guide these monsters in their actions, which ultimately forces the characters to decide how to triage the unexpected outbreak and get to the bottom of the mystery. Pilhua does not have an inn or tavern in the traditional sense and instead accommodates visitors in the **Common House** described in **Part One** of the adventure. The sequence of events unfolds in the following order: **Murder of Cacalotls**, **Wight Night**, and **Purple Maize**. After these three activities take place (or two if the characters circumvented the **Murder of Cacalotls** as explained in the preceding **Ciahuatl** section), the adventure's focus shifts to the maizefield, which is the ultimate source of the ills plaguing Pilhua. You are free to determine the exact timing of the preceding encounters, though it is suggested to give the characters enough time to recoup and heal before another enemy descends upon Pilhua and points the heroes in the direction of the maizefield.

Murder of Cacalotls

Frustrated and angry about the lack of progress in solving the missing teenagers' disappearance, Conto's fiancée Ciahuatl unleashes her band of **8 cacalotls** upon the person whose futility has led her to this decision: Papalotl. Shortly after nightfall, the constructs leave their posts in the fields and coalesce around their leader Ciahuatl, who directs the monsters toward the Temple of Tonacayotl to punish the people of Pilhua for their inaction and ineptitude in locating her lost lover. When the cacalotls first appear in the village, read or paraphrase the following description:

> The pale moonlight reveals the terrifying silhouettes of eight shambling monstrosities crafted from cloth and straw that bear sharp claws at the tips of their scrawny, fibrous fingers. The creatures fan out across the village in an apparent search for something or someone. A young woman wearing a black skirt and blouse trails behind them.

A character who already met Ciahuatl can identify her as the woman trailing behind the cacalotls. Otherwise, the woman's identity remains unknown. Conto's distraught widow targets Papalotl whom she presumes is somewhere near the Temple of Tonacayotl where the nobles live and socialize. When the cacalotls arrive on the scene, **Papalotl** and **4 jaguar warriors** stand ready to meet them. If Cintecuhtli, the priest of Tonacayotl, is nearby, he sees his role as tending to the injured and does not join the combat.

Throughout the battle, the unhinged Ciahuatl bitterly complains about Papalotl's incompetence, screaming that he could not locate a priest in a temple or an ear of maize in a maizefield.

She also repeatedly screams, "Where is my Conto? Where is my Conto?" Her irrational ranting borders on being delusional as her valid criticisms quickly devolve into blaming him for the sun setting in the evening and the rains not falling on command. In the span of a few minutes, the distraught young woman heaps an entire year of repressed emotions and grievances on the man she holds responsible for not taking enough action to find her beloved Conto and his younger sister.

If the characters intervene in her plans for revenge, they can attempt to verbally convince her to call off her assault as described in the **Speaking with Ciahuatl** sidebar found in **Part One**, though Ciahuatil has only a 35% chance of listening to them if they do so at this late juncture. Despite focusing her attention on Papalotl, she retaliates against a character who attacks her. Ciahuatl never surrenders unless a character successfully convinces her otherwise as discussed in the **Speaking with Ciahuatl** sidebar and only provides information to the characters that appears in that section. If someone kills her, she passionately proclaims her joy at being reunited with her true love and her loathing for the people who failed them during their abbreviated lives.

Cacalotls (8): HD 4; HP 28, 25, 24, 21, 19x2, 17, 16; AC 9[10]; Atk 2 claws (1d6 + poison); Move 12; Save 13; AL C; CL/XP 5/240; **Special:** camouflage (when motionless, appears as ordinary doll or scarecrow), cackle (1/day, 30ft radius, save or 2d6 damage and frightened as *fear* spell, save for half damage and avoids fear), darkvision (60ft), poison (save or additional 1d4 damage), vulnerable to fire (200% damage). (see **Appendix A: New Monsters**)

Ciahuatl, Female Aztli Human: HD 8; HP 28; AC 9[10] or 2[17] (missile) and 4[15] (melee) from *shield* spell; Atk tecpatl (1d6); Move 12; Save 8; AL N (but becoming C); CL/XP 9/1100; **Special:** baleful melancholy (3/day, 30ft radius, target must save or suffer –1 penalty to hit, saves, and armor class for 1 hour), crushing despair (1/day, 30ft radius, save or 2d6 damage from crushing despair, save for half), darkvision (60ft), immune to charm and fear, spells (4/3/3/2 MU), twisted thoughts (anyone reading her mind must save or become frightened as *fear* spell) **Spells:** 1st—*charm person, magic missile, shield, sleep;* 2nd—*darkness 15ft radius, invisibility, mirror image;* 3rd—*hold person, lightning bolt, suggestion;* 4th—*confusion, fear.* **Equipment:** tecpatl[B].

Jaguar Warriors, Male or Female Aztli Humans (17): HD 1; AC 8[11]; Atk itztopillis (1d6); Move 12; Save 17; AL Any; CL/XP 1/15; **Special:** none. (***Monstrosities*** 257) **Equipment:** ichcahuipilli armor[B], itztopilli[B].

Papalotl, Male Aztli Human (Ftr4): HP 28; AC 4[15]; Atk macuahuitl (1d8); Move 12; Save 14; AL N; CL/XP 4/120; **Special:** multiple attacks (4) vs. creatures with 1 or fewer HD. **Equipment:** ollixalli armor[B], macuahuitl[B].

[B] See **Appendix B: New Items and Magic**

Wight Night

Shortly after the tumult of the cacalotl attacks dies down, or if the characters successfully convinced Ciahuatl not to attack Pilhua, the next vengeful act gets its turn on the stage. If the characters decided to spend the night at the **Common House**, Mixoch and Temilaz also made the same choice this evening, bringing the characters directly into the action. Alternatively, the pair may be spending the night at a nearby nobleperson's home when another frightening cry rings through the village. The sword wight commences its hunt for his killers at the **Common House** where Uetzopilli most commonly encountered them during the overnight hours. In response to the evening's earlier activities, Papalotl, if he survived, posts 2 jaguar warriors as sentries to prevent further attacks. Unfortunately, 1d3 hours later, his worst fears come true when Uetzopilli returns to Pilhua as a **sword wight** accompanied by **8 gnoll zombies** under his command. When Uetzopilli and his gang arrive in the village, read or paraphrase the following description:

> The stench of death accompanies a withering, desiccated corpse wielding a vicious macuahuitl wrapped in leathery, decaying flesh in its bony hands. A team of animated gnoll corpses loiter around him as the obviously undead abomination shambles forward to slay the living and add its victims to its swelling ranks.

If Mixoch and Temilaz are present when the undead attack, the enraged sword wight points at the pair and wryly smiles while twirling the macuahuitl in its bony hands. It screams, "Remember me? You dumped me in that wretched hole, but here I am again. Say hello, boys, for I am only the messenger. Wait until you see what else awaits this disgusting village!"

A character who looks at the pochtecas notices that they obviously recognize the undead monstrosity and appear very worried. The murderers naturally turn to their newfound "allies" for help and beg them to stop the undead horror they claim they first encountered rising from its grave several months ago. Of course, the sword wight refuses to let this lie go unchallenged and promptly refutes the pair's claim and insists that they also killed the missing children. Uetzopilli insists that they can see for themselves with a trip to the maizefield north-northwest of Pilhua.

The characters are free to let Uetzopilli and his zombies exact their revenge against the pair, but the sword wight and his minions turn their attention to the heroes when they finish with their original targets. Uetzopilli shows no mercy to his killers, swinging at them until he and his minions savagely butcher them.

If Mixoch and Temilaz survive their close call with the sword wight, they steadfastly deny Uetzopilli's allegations, although their resolve starts to crack if the characters threaten to go to the original crime scene in the maizefield right now, and they might possibly divulge the details of their murderous actions more than one year earlier if threatened. For more details about interacting with the pochtecas, refer to the **Speaking with Mixoch and Temilaz** sidebar.

The sword wight and his zombie minions left a trail leading from the maizefield into the village.

Sword Wight: HD 8; **HP** 48; **AC** 4[15]; **Atk** macuahuitl (1d8 + level drain) or slam (1d4 + level drain); **Move** 9; **Save** 8; **AL** C; **CL/XP** 10/1400; **Special:** +1 or better magic or silver weapons to hit, darkvision (60ft), level drain (1 level with hit, save avoids). (see **Appendix A: New Monsters**)
Equipment: ollixalli armor[B], macuahuitl[B], gold and sapphire circlet (100 gp value).

Gnoll Zombies (8): HD 2; **HP** 15, 14, 12x3, 11x2, 9; **AC** 8[11]; **Atk** strike (1d8); **Move** 6; **Save** 16; **AL** N; **CL/XP** 2/30; **Special:** immune to sleep and charm. (*Monstrosities* 529)
[B] See **Appendix B: New Items and Magic**

PURPLE MAIZE

After the two initial encounters within the village, the action shifts outside the village proper and into the outskirts where the characters run across the culprit responsible for Zihuia's murder. The characters by now have several potential clues that point them in that direction, including obtaining information and a confession from Mixoch and Temilaz, accompanying Ciahuatl to the maizefield, following up on Uetzopilli's statements about the maizefield, or following the trail the sword wight and his minions left back to their origin. If the characters still appear stuck on where to go next, you can use Cintecuhtli to tend to their injuries and also provide some additional insight he gained about the evils plaguing the village. This additional insight may directly point the characters in the maizefield's direction or provide a more roundabout means of getting them there. If Venlo is tagging along with the characters, he may also serve as an informational resource for them.

Travel through the village requires the heroes to traverse the maizefields and farms scattered across the settlement's breadth. While traipsing through this landscape of towering maize interspersed with wild grasses and cereal grains, the heroes come upon **2 wahuapas** concealed among the ordinary maize plants. When the characters move within striking range of the creatures, read or paraphrase the following description:

Two maize plants suddenly uproot their tendrilled, fibrous legs from the loose soil and lurch forward, displaying their sharp serrated leaves in an obvious attacking position. One ear of maize at the top of the plant's central stalk seems to function as its crude brain, though the monstrosity lacks eyes, ears, or any other discernible sensory organ or orifice.

The monsters are incapable of speech or profound tactics. They wade into combat swinging their sharpened leaves like scythes mowing through rows of wheat. If the characters charge them, one monster uses its entangle ability to slow down the adventurers. Otherwise, the creatures fight until destroyed, ultimately clearing the adventurers' path to the maizefield. The wahuapas may be sentient, but their intellects are child-like. If the characters can magically communicate with them, the monsters are limited to conveying simple concepts, though the plant that killed Zihuia acknowledges committing the crime in basic terms. A character who searches the nearby area discovers two holes in the ground identical to those found in the maizefield outside of Zihuia's house, thus confirming the wahuapa occupied the spot before the killing. The monsters have no treasure or personal belongings.

Wahuapa (Maizefolk) (2): HD 7; **HP** 54, 50; **AC** 7[12]; **Atk** 2 claws (1d6 + blood meal); **Move** 9; **Save** 9; **AL** N; **CL/XP** 8/800; **Special:** blood meal (save or additional 1d4 damage, wahuapa gains hp equal to damage), camouflage (1-in-6 chance to spot while standing still in maizefield), entangle (3/day, plants grow in 10ft radius within range, save or restrained, Open Doors check to escape). (see **Appendix A: New Monsters**)

Part Three: The Haunted Maizefield

Roughly 1–1/2 miles north-northwest of Pilhua stands the maizefield, the malevolent creation of Conto and Chipinia who now haunt the dreaded maze as a pair of unrequiteds, a melancholy brood of incorporeal undead. The vengeful creatures contorted the maize plants surrounding their makeshift grave into a solid yet not impenetrable barrier of fibrous plant materials. Despite its unnatural, magical manipulation, the plants are still alive and resistant to flames if the heroes try to burn the siblings' strange creation to the ground. Inside its walls, the teenagers shaped their lair into a confounding maze replete with dead-ends and trapped passageways to ensnare trespassers and amuse the wicked duo. When the characters get within visual range of the locale, read or paraphrase the following description:

Twisted stalks of maize, husks, vines, and leaves create a formidable yet not solid barrier around the perimeter and canopy of a circular structure roughly 220 feet in diameter and 15 feet high near the center of the creation. There is no visible entrance or breach in its outer wall or ceiling to access what lies behind its greenish curtain. The grassland surrounding the stronghold appears still and devoid of wildlife save for the occasional drone of a flying pest or distant birdcall.

If not for its baleful origins, the haunted maizefield would be a wondrous diversion from life's drudgeries. The roughly circular, enclosed wall of maize resembles the shape of a modern-day circus big top as the husks, stalks, and leaves intertwine to form a barrier that blocks line of sight. Its walls are five feet thick and reach a height of 10 feet. The structure's roof reaches an apex of 15 feet at its center and tapers off to 10 feet along the edges, though it is only two feet thick. The characters can move through the wall, though their movement is one-quarter their normal rate. The maize wall is an object that can be damaged and thus breached. It has AC 8[11] and 50 hit points per 10-foot section (20 hit points for the roof) and is immune to blunt weapons, but is vulnerable to slashing damage (double damage). Reducing a 10-foot section of maize to 0 hit points destroys it, though the maize complex retains its structural integrity.

Maizefield Features

The interior of the maizefield has similar dimensions to its exterior though, like the ceiling, the walls are only two feet thick rather than five feet thick, thus requiring only 20 points of damage to breach an interior wall. The ceiling is 10 feet high along the outer edges and then 1d4 + 10 feet high inside the outermost concentric ring. Unless the characters create a breach in the ceiling or outer walls, no light penetrates inside the maze, shrouding the interior in darkness. The absence of light prohibits the growth of any grasses or other vegetation between the maize rows that grow from the ground to the roof. A character who looks for tracks finds only sporadic humanoid footprints mostly in the outermost concentric rings. The inner rings seem curiously devoid of any noteworthy impressions in the ground.

The menagerie of creatures inhabiting the maze are not confined to one location, with the exception of the monsters in **Areas M5** and **M6**. The siblings' spirits exert control only over the wahuapas and limited mastery over the tear collector. The remaining denizens are generally free-willed and move through the maze unimpeded, though they tend to stay away from the preceding locations. They fail to coordinate any organized response to intruders, with every inhabitant fending for itself unless an opportunity to feed or kill another creature falls into its lap. For every five minutes spent inside the maze, there is a 50% chance of one of the following encounters occurring. The randomly encountered monsters are also found in a keyed location within the maze. You may subtract any monsters the characters face here from those listed in the detailed area.

Table 1–2: Maze Random Encounters

d6	Encounter
1	1d3 bilwises (see **Area M2**)
2	1d4 ghouls (see **Area M1**)
3	1 raggedy man (see **Area M4**)
4–6	Vision (see below)

Vision

A random character must succeed on a saving throw or become incapacitated while momentarily experiencing a horrifying vision that lasts for 1d4 rounds. Consult **Table 1–3** below to determine what the character hears and sees during this re-enactment. A character cannot experience the same vision twice.

Table 1–3: Visions within the Maze

d4	Vision Experienced
1	**Prelude:** A teenage boy and girl lie in a field looking up at the sky while smoking tobacco and drinking pulque. A loud commotion ensues somewhere in the distance, causing the children to get up and quietly creep through the maize to investigate it.
2	**Crime:** A teenage boy and girl hide behind maize stalks, intently watching two men and a half-elf argue about an undetermined subject. The half-elf falls to his knees and grovels as the two men plunge their tecpatls into his chest and slice his throat. The teenage boy and girl loudly scream, drawing the men's attention to them. A character who experiences this vision identifies the killers as Mixoch and Temilaz, provided the individual already met them during the course of the adventure.
3	**Murder:** Two men race toward a teenage boy and girl, who momentarily freeze. The men jump on top of them, stabbing them mercilessly with their tecpatls and slicing their throats as they helplessly scream. The teenagers fall to the ground limp, though one of the culprits broke his tecpatl blade. A character who experiences this vision identifies the killers as Mixoch and Temilaz, provided the individual already met them during the course of the adventure. That person also recognizes Mixoch as the person who broke his tecpatl.
4	**Aftermath:** Two men dump the bodies of a slain half-elf, a teenage boy, and a teenage girl into a pit in the middle of a remote maizefield. They hurriedly fill the hole with earth and transplant a maize plant on top of the crude grave to further conceal its location. A character who experiences this vision identifies the men digging the hole as Mixoch and Temilaz, provided the individual already met them during the course of the adventure.

Area T: Traps

In addition to the malevolent denizens who prowl the maze, the siblings' corporeal minions also created devious mechanical devices to ensnare the unwary. Four of them are scattered throughout the complex as shown on the accompanying map. The type of trap is not designated on the map, and you are free to use any of the following traps or a combination of them.

THE HAUNTED MAIZEFIELD
T
M3
W
W
T
M2
M5
M4
M6
W
W
T
M1
W
N
1 Square – 10 Feet

Popcorn Trap

A pressure plate in the ground at the spot marked "T" pressurizes hardened kernels of popcorn hidden within faux husks interspersed among the neighboring maize stalks. A creature who weighs more than 50 pounds that steps on the pressure plate triggers the trap.

When the trap is triggered, all creatures within 10 feet of the pressure plate take 3d6 points of damage from the impact of being struck by the dried kernels, which function like shrapnel. The creature takes half as much damage on a successful save. When the husks explode, there is a 50% chance that a monster from **Table 1–2** comes to investigate the commotion within 1d4 rounds of the explosion.

Falling Maize Trap

This devious trap uses a tripwire to cause two wooden poles on opposite walls to fall forward and strike the creature who disturbed the trip wire.

The thin wire is three inches off the ground, and the wooden poles are disguised as maize stalks that are supported by a hinge mechanism that causes each to fall parallel to the tripwire. The trap activates when a creature hits the tripwire. Each wooden pole, which has razor-sharp obsidian shards embedded into its surface, attacks as a 5HD creature against the target who triggered the trap or is standing adjacent to the tripwire, doing 3d6 points of damage (or half as much with a successful saving throw). Each pole hits the creature closest to it, and the same pole cannot strike more than one creature.

Teleportation Trap

A pressure plate hidden in the ground at the spot marked "T" activates this magical trap. A living creature that steps on the pressure plate and weighs more than 50 pounds triggers the trap. The target must succeed on a saving throw or be instantly teleported to a random location 1d6 x 10 feet away from the pressure plate. Because the maize wall is an object, a creature transported into a maize wall appears in an unoccupied space adjacent to the maize wall that is closest to the pressure plate. A spell or other effect that can sense the presence of magic, such as *detect magic*, reveals an aura of magic around the pressure plate.

Area W: Wahuapa

Naturally, a maze created from maize also contains wahuapas that blend into the wall and serve as an added line of defense against intruders. These points in the maze designated as "W" are the locations where each of the **4 wahuapas** hide within the structure. Characters searching the maze have a 1-in-6 chance of noticing the creatures lurking amid the ordinary plants that make up the semi-solid barrier. When a creature passes within 10 feet of one of these monsters, the maizefolk emerges from the wall and attacks, likely surprising the interloper in the process. The wahuapa fights until destroyed. If a character attempts to communicate with one of these plants, it reacts in the same manner as described in the **Purple Maize** encounter.

Wahuapa (Maizefolk): HD 7; AC 7[12]; Atk 2 claws (1d6 + blood meal); **Move** 9; **Save** 9; **AL** N; **CL/XP** 8/800; **Special:** blood meal (save or additional 1d4 damage, wahuapa gains hp equal to damage), camouflage (1-in-6 chance to spot while standing still in maizefield), entangle (3/day, plants grow in 10ft radius within range, save or restrained, Open Doors check to escape). (see **Appendix A: New Monsters**)

Area M1: Ghoulish Delight

These shambling, undead monstrosities congregate in a dead-end in the outermost concentric ring forming the maze. They are the Haunted Maizefield's newest additions, though they frequently enter and exit the structure searching for living prey beyond its boundaries. When the characters come within visual range of their disgusting corner, read or paraphrase the following description:

The filth can be attributed to **6 ghouls** that inhabit this area of the maze on an apparently temporary basis. The monsters are fairly mobile and move about the complex as well as venturing out of it. Without leadership and direction, the undead horrors mob any creature that wanders into their corner of the maze. They fight without fear, never retreating nor surrendering. If the characters can communicate with the ghouls, they know nothing about the maze's inner workings.

Ghouls (6): HD 2; HP 15, 13x2, 12, 10x2; AC 6[13]; **Atk** 2 claws (1d3 + paralysis), bite (1d4); **Move** 9; **Save** 16; **AL** C; **CL/XP** 3/60; **Special:** immunities (charm and sleep), paralyzing touch (3d6 turns, save avoids). (**Monstrosities** 191)

Treasure: The ghouls amassed a few baubles among their mounds of refuse, though it takes some digging to locate a pouch containing 28 cacao beans worth 1 gp each and a *potion of healing*.

Area M2: Fields of Maize Silk

The vengeful energies of the maizefield summoned these elementals to this forsaken location where they move about the field waiting to slaughter unwanted visitors. The creatures appear to be crafted from the same fibrous plant materials as the wahuapas, which may lead the characters to conclude they share some common ancestry or origin, but the wispy monsters lack the physical substance of the malevolent maizefolk. Despite their seemingly incorporeal nature, they are not skilled at blending into the vegetation or noticing intruders. A character who succeeds on a saving throw feels a slight breeze emanating from the nearby gap in the wall. When the characters approach this juncture in the maze, read or paraphrase the following description:

The **5 bilwises** who inhabit this portion of the maze are remnants from an ancient farmer's long-forgotten grudge. However, they seamlessly blended into the siblings' plans for the site and now reside among their evil brethren. When the monsters notice the characters, they fly forward to attack, moving through the walls to allow some of their ranks to get behind the heroes and flank them. During the first round of combat, each bilwis uses its whirlwind ability to knock its adversaries off their feet. The elementals then slam the characters into submission.

If the characters reduce the bilwises' numbers in half, the remaining survivors attempt to flee by flying through the ceiling and into the wilderness outside the maizefield. The monster hides out for several hours before returning to the maizefield to ensure the safety of their accumulated treasures hidden in the surrounding walls. The bilwises' knowledge of the maizefield is limited to the outer concentric rings, though they know a terrible crime took place here and that the resurrected spirits of the children and the man slain here rose from the grave.

Bilwis (5): HD 6; HP 38, 35, 34, 30, 29; AC 6[13]; **Atk** slam (1d8); **Move** 12 (fly); **Save** 11; **AL** C; **CL/XP** 8/800; **Special:** whirlwind (1/day, 5ft radius, 2d6 damage and knocked prone, save for half and remain standing). (see **Appendix A: New Monsters**)
Treasure: The bilwises keep a scroll of *pyrotechnics* and a *cuacalalatli of the beast (eagle)* (see **Appendix B: New Items and Magic**) hidden within the maize.

Area M3: Fun Guys

Maize is susceptible to fungi and even the magically manipulated plants that form this enclosure are no exception. If the characters pass through this section of the maze, **8 phycomids** growing in this section detect their approach. Although the fungi initially developed on the plant stalks and leaves, they slowly migrated into the loose soil between the maize walls where they wait for passing prey. When the characters come within visual range of this area, read or paraphrase the following description if a character is examining the maize.

If a character takes the time to examine the vegetation, that individual determines that the grasses are indeed yellowy strands of fungi. If a creature moves within 10 feet of the phycomids, the monsters uproot themselves from the soil and move forward to attack, lobbing fluid globules at their enemies. The unintelligent phycomids attack until destroyed.

Phycomid: HD 4; AC 4[15]; **Atk** acid fluid globule (1d6 + spore infection); **Move** 3; **Save** 13; **AL** N; **CL/XP** 5/240; **Special:** acid fluid globule (20ft ranged attack, save or spore infection), spore infection (save or lose 1d2 constitution immediately and 1 point constitution every 10 minutes, cure disease heals, dies at 0 constitution and forms new phycomid patch). (see **Appendix A: New Monsters**)

Area M4: Rags to Ditches

Much like the cacalotls encountered earlier, the inhabitants of this section of the maze appear to be creepy, yet harmless inanimate objects. The monsters conceal themselves well among the vegetation in the ceiling above the breach, giving the characters a 1-in-6 chance to notice them, or a 3-in-6 chance if they state that they are specifically looking at the ceiling. When the characters come within visual range of this breach, read or paraphrase the following description:

If a character noticed the objects in the ceiling, you may add the following detail:

There are **4 raggedy men** hidden among the vegetation at this critical breach in the maize wall. The devious aberrations attempt to pass themselves off as discarded children's dolls. Indeed, a character who hails from Pilhua notices a striking similarity between the creature and a style of doll popular in the village. However, it is impossible to determine if the creature was once Chipinia's toy that somehow came to life or if the resemblance is a curious coincidence. Regardless, the cunning monsters take advantage of this perception and use their beguiling gaze attack while still affixed to the canopy to charm as many opponents as they can before hurling their gossamer strands at characters who resist their charm effect. They spend as long as possible attached to their target before dropping to the ground to attack. Despite their cleverness, the monsters are mindless lifeforms that subsist on sapping the vitality of other creatures. The concepts of death, wealth, and motivation do not register with raggedy man's alien mindset. The creatures attack the characters until destroyed.

Raggedy Men (4): HD 4; HP 20, 27, 25, 21; AC 2[17]; **Atk** slam (1d6) or gossamer strand (1d4 + life drain); **Move** 12; **Save** 13; **AL** C; **CL/XP** 5/240; **Special:** beguiling gaze (3/day, 30ft range, as *charm person*, save avoids, charmed target automatically hit by gossamer strand attack), gossamer strand (30ft ranged attack, inflicts life drain on next round), immune to blunt weapons, life drain (automatic 1d4 damage, raggedy man gains damage amount as hit points), vulnerable to fire (200%). (see **Appendix A: New Monsters**)

Area M5: Drowning in Sorrow

Under extraordinary circumstances, a child's profound tears of sadness can sometimes spawn unintended consequences. When Conto and Chipinia met their terrifying demise at Mixoch and Temilaz's hands, the tears they shed took on a life of their own as a wicked **tear collector**. The small fiend appears as a humanoid-shaped creature chiseled from rock salt. It dwells at the heart of the maze, likely leading the characters to conclude that it is the cause of the mayhem plaguing the Pilhua. To get inside this section of the maizefield, the heroes must push through the walls or ceiling granting access to the area. When they do so, read or paraphrase the following description:

The tear collector loiters near the shallow pool, which is only a few inches deep and contains saline water that feels granular to the touch because of the exceedingly high salt content. The **2 bloodsuckle bushes** also burrow their roots into the pool's banks even though the plants subsist on blood and meat that the tear collector provides it from its available sources. The tear collector watches over the bushes. When he sees creatures approach the pool, he blasts the trespassers with a cone of acidic tears. The plants then grab at the characters with their tendrils.

Throughout the encounter, the tear collector weeps, sobs, and wails about the injustice committed upon "them" and the "terror of the earth." The fiend further mopes about youth being stolen and the indignity of being shoved into an unmarked grave for no good reason. Despite its excessive lamentation, the monster remains focused on killing the characters and recreating the raw emotions the teenagers experienced during their final moments alive. If the characters converse with the tear collector about the murdered teenagers or any other subject pertaining to the maizefield and its occupants, it blurts out, "fate breathed life into their pathetic spirits and stirred their hatred into palpable anger. Greed sowed these fruits of wrath." The fiend otherwise refuses to respond to their questions and provides no further explanation regarding its statement about the perils of avarice. The characters can magically compel it to reply, in which case it reveals Conto and Chipinia's sad story in exacting details as well as their current location within the maze. However, the tear collector has little knowledge of the other creatures inhabiting its lair. The creature's bond to the locale prevents it from fleeing when faced with imminent destruction.

Tear Collector: HD 6; HP 40; AC 5[14]; **Atk** corrosive touch (2d4); **Move** 12 (swim 12); **Save** 11; **AL** C; **CL/XP** 8/800; **Special:** +1 or better magic weapons to hit, acid tears (3/day, 15ft cone, 2d6 damage, save for half), immune to acid and fire. (see **Appendix A: New Monsters**)

Bloodsuckle Bushes (2): HD 6; HP 41, 36; AC 7[12]; **Atk** 2 tendrils (1d4), limb rake (1d6); **Move** 0 (immobile); **Save** 11; **AL** N; **CL/XP** 8/800; **Special:** blood drain (if 2 tendrils hit target, grab and automatic 1d4 damage per round), create host (1/month, inject seed, host dies in 1d4 days), inject sap (save or held as *charm person*), summon host (sound draws nearby hosts). (see **Appendix A: New Monsters**)
Treasure: A character can discover recently disturbed soil around the pool's edge. If a creature excavates the area, the individual recovers a wooden box containing a *potion of extra healing*, a *potion of giant strength*, a *stone of stunning*[B], a jar of tlilitl[B], and seven garnets worth 100 gp each.
[B] See **Appendix B: New Items and Magic**

Area M6: Unrequited

One year after their deaths, the teenagers' spirits were reborn as undead monstrosities known as unrequiteds. The youngsters whose blood gave birth to the wahuapas and whose tears conjured the tear collector have no recollection of their former lives. They cannot relay the circumstances of their deaths to the characters and now exist solely to slay every creature that stands in their way. The incorporeal beings appear as wispy, crimson vapors that periodically

take the form of an adolescent humanoid. If the characters approach Conto and Chipinia's grave, read or paraphrase the following description:

> Several mounds of disinterred earth lie along the outline of a carefully dug hole where the surprisingly well-preserved corpses of a young man and young woman rest atop each other at the bottom. The stench of freshly removed earth and decay linger in the air.

The siblings' spirits transcended their earthly bodies and transformed into **2 unrequiteds** that loiter around the grave where Mixoch and Temilaz dumped them more than one year ago alongside Uetzopilli. The incorporeal monsters pass through the maize walls and ceiling without impediment, which allows them to freely move about the area. The pair use the maize walls to their advantage to physically strike at the characters with their debilitating touch. Regardless of the circumstances, they never venture more than 50 feet from their grave and cannot recount any details about their untimely deaths. The siblings can speak, but they limit their conversations to threatening statements and wild boasts.

The apparitions are susceptible to effects that force them to laugh or experience other joyful emotions, which partially accounts for their reluctance to speak. While they never laugh of their own accord, the characters can forcibly compel them to do so by casting spells and magical effects that make them laugh. As previously stated, they remember nothing about their mortal existence and instead focus their malevolent energies on expanding their territory and slaying humanoids. The undead apparitions fight to the end, attacking the heroes mercilessly until they kill their quarry or until the characters end their unnatural existence.

If the characters defeat the ghostly siblings, they are free to explore the grave and retrieve their bodies. Despite being buried for an entire year in a temperate climate with ample moisture, the corpses remain virtually pristine with only mild signs of decomposition. A character who examines the bodies can determine that each sustained puncture wounds to the chest and slashing injuries to the neck. They wear the same clothes they wore on the day they vanished. Characters can also locate a broken tecpatl blade and its intact handle. Even casual scrutiny of the weapon reveals that the handle is shaped into the likeness of an ocelot poised to pounce. The weapon belonged to Mixoch, a fact characters can confirm by showing or describing the object to villagers who regularly frequent Pilhua's marketplace.

Despite being incorporeal, the ghostly spirits amassed some items that Uetzopilli's zombie minions hid under the mounds of dirt adjacent to their graves. It is impossible to locate their riches without disturbing the earth.

Conto and Chipinia, Unrequiteds (2): HD 6; HP 45, 39; AC 5[14]; **Atk** baleful touch (1d8 + level drain); **Move** 12 (fly); **Save** 11; **AL** C; **CL/XP** 8/800; **Special:** +1 or better magic weapons to hit, level drain (1 level with touch, save avoids), incorporeal, mournful glare (1/day, 60ft radius, save or movement halved and −1 penalty to attacks and saves for 1d4+1 rounds), resistances (cold, electricity, fire) (50% damage). (see **Appendix A: New Monsters**)
Treasure: Uncovering the loose soil around the grave reveals a golden jaguar statue worth 1,000 gp, a *tangled gourd*[B], a *rope of climbing*, and *war paint (orange)*[B].
- See **Appendix B: New Items and Magic**

CONCLUDING THE ADVENTURE

In the aftermath of the unrequiteds' destruction, the maizefield slowly unravels over the next several days as the leaves and stalks forming the roof steadily wane and the walls come undone. The remaining wahuapas go their separate ways to further terrorize Pilhua or other neighboring villages until they are rooted out and vanquished once and for all. If the characters return Conto and Chipinia to the village, Cintecuhtli gives them a proper burial, which gives their grieving family an answer to their long-simmering questions and some measure of closure surrounding their untimely deaths.

If the characters have not already identified Mixoch and Temilaz as the teenagers' killers, the discovery of Mixoch's missing, broken weapon inside the youngsters' grave offers ample proof of at least his guilt. When faced with this evidence, Papalotl has no choice but to dispense the village's brand of frontier justice on the pair or to turn them over to Ixtla's representatives for suitable punishment. The grateful Ciahuatl, if she still lives and if the characters turned her away from evil, profusely thanks the characters for their efforts and dedicates her life to protecting the innocent from harm.

In appreciation for their actions, Pilhua holds a great feast and celebration to honor the heroes who saved their community and unmasked the criminals who perpetrated the horrific crime that set these unfortunately events into motion.

The following new monsters appear in the adventures in the book:

BILWIS

Hit Dice: 6
Armor Class: 6[13]
Attacks: slam (1d8)
Saving Throw: 11
Special: whirlwind
Move: 12 (fly)
Alignment: Chaos
Number Encountered: 1 or 1d4
Challenge Level/XP: 8/800

A bilwis appears as a wavering outline of a person, its outline marked by grass and weeds that flow about it as if caught on a breeze. The creature's form is mirage-like and wavers as it moves. Bilwises are elemental creatures sometimes referred to as "field ghosts" often found inhabiting fields of maize. Bilwises slam their opponents, but once per day they can unleash a dangerous whirlwind in a five-foot radius about their wavering forms that does 2d6 points of damage and knocks creatures prone. A target can make a saving throw for half damage and to remain standing.

Bilwis: HD 6; AC 6[13]; **Atk** slam (1d8); **Move** 12 (fly); **Save** 11; AL C; **CL/XP** 8/800; **Special:** whirlwind (1/day, 5ft radius, 2d6 damage and knocked prone, save for half and remain standing).

BLOODSUCKLE BUSH

Hit Dice: 6
Armor Class: 7[12]
Attacks: 2 tendrils (1d4), limb rake (1d6)
Saving Throw: 11
Special: blood drain, create host, seed, summon host
Move: 0 (immobile)
Alignment: Neutrality
Number Encountered: 1 or 1d4
Challenge Level/XP: 8/800

A bloodsuckle is a nightmarish bush consisting of a bulbous root from which sprout several vine-like tendrils. The tendrils end in hollow, needlelike points and can reach lengths of 60 feet. Woody limbs as thick as a human's leg sprout from the trunk of the bloodsuckle. The leaves of a bloodsuckle bush are a vile greenish color, and constantly ooze a sticky sap that reeks of decay, filth, and other unmentionable odors. Bloodsuckles are semi-intelligent, immobile plants that gain nourishment from the blood of living creatures. Once per day, a bloodsuckle can inject its sap into a host using its tendrils so it can control the creature to attack others or approach the plant to drain its blood. If a bloodsuckle hits a victim with both tendrils, it automatically begins draining the creature's blood (1d4 hit points per round). Once per month, a bloodsuckle can generate a walnut-sized seed that it implant's in a host's body. The host is then sent away, and a new bloodsuckle sprouts in the victim in 1d4 days. If threatened, the bloodsuckle can produce a high-pitched whine that draws nearby hosts to defend it.

Bloodsuckle Bush: HD 6; AC 7[12]; **Atk** 2 tendrils (1d4), limb rake (1d6); **Move** 0 (immobile); **Save** 11; AL N; **CL/XP** 8/800; **Special:** blood drain (if 2 tendrils hit target, grab and automatic 1d4 damage per round), create host (1/month, inject seed, host dies in 1d4 days), inject sap (save or held as *charm person*), summon host (sound draws nearby hosts).

CACALOTL

Hit Dice: 4
Armor Class: 9[10]
Attack: 2 claws (1d6 + poison)
Special: camouflage, cackle, darkvision, poison, vulnerable to fire
Move: 12
Saving Throw: 13
Alignment: Chaos
Number Encountered: 1, 1d4, 2d8
Challenge Level/XP: 5/240

Cacalotls are shambling monstrosities crafted from cloth and straw that bear sharp claws at the tips of their scrawny, fibrous fingers. They appear to be scarecrows, which they are indistinguishable from when motionless. They attack with their poisoned claws, which deal an additional 1d4 points of damage to a creature that fails a saving throw. Once per day, a cacalotl can cackle, causing all creatures within 30 feet to take 2d6 points of damage and be frightened (as a *fear* spell). A creature that makes its saving throw takes half damage from the cackle and resists being frightened.

Cacalotl: HD 4; AC 9[10]; **Atk** 2 claws (1d6 + poison); **Move** 12; **Save** 13; AL C; **CL/XP** 5/240; **Special:** camouflage (when motionless, appears as ordinary doll or scarecrow), cackle (1/day, 30ft radius, 2d6 damage and frightened as *fear* spell, save for half damage and avoids fear), darkvision (60ft), poison (save or additional 1d4 damage), vulnerable to fire (200% damage).

PHYCOMID

Hit Dice: 4
Armor Class: 4[15]
Attack: Acid fluid globule (1d6 + spore infection)
Saving Throw: 13
Special: Acid, spore infection
Move: 3
Alignment: Neutrality
Challenge Level/XP: 5/240

A patch of phycomids is often found growing in garbage heaps, refuse, and other such places. A typical patch of phycomid covers an area of two feet. The actual number of mushroom-growths varies with the actual size of the patch. The mushroom caps are usually white, red, purple, or yellow in color, and the phycomid's body is milky white.

The phycomid attacks by extruding a small tube from its body and firing a glob of acid at a foe. The phycomid can fire a globule up to 20 feet. A creature hit by a phycomid's fluid globule attack must succeed on a saving throw or lose 1d2 points of constitution as tiny mushroom-like growths sprout from its body.

Every 10 minutes thereafter, the character loses 1 point of constitution until he or she receives a *cure disease* spell. At constitution 0, the victim dies and his body collapses to the ground, where a new phycomid patch sprouts. Lost points of constitution return at the rate of 1 point per day of rest.

Phycomid: HD 4; AC 4[15]; **Atk** acid fluid globule (1d6 + spore infection); **Move** 3; **Save** 13; AL N; **CL/XP** 5/240; **Special:** acid fluid globule (20ft ranged attack, save or spore infection), spore infection (save or lose 1d2 constitution immediately and 1 point constitution every 10 minutes, cure disease heals, dies at 0 constitution and forms new phycomid patch).

RAGGEDY MAN

Hit Dice: 4
Armor Class: 2[17]
Attack: slam (1d6)
Saving Throw: 13
Special: Beguiling gaze, gossamer strand, life drain, immune to blunt weapons, vulnerable to fire
Move: 12
Alignment: Neutrality
Challenge Level/XP: 5/240

A raggedy man appears to be a tattered doll made of linen and stuffed with grasses and maize stalks. Twine is used to keep their stuffing inside their small forms. These tiny terrors absorb violent death to gain a malevolent intelligence. They often wait to be picked up and then strike their target with a powerful slam. More often, however, they attack their foe with a gossamer strand of twine launched from 30 feet away. If this strand hits, the target initially takes 1d4 points of damage and continues taking 1d4 points of damage each round thereafter until the strand is cut. A target can cut the strand by taking a round to do so or by moving more than 30 feet away from the raggedy man (which follows its victim to stay close). The raggedy man gains any damage done to the target as hit points.

Once per day, a raggedy man can use its beguiling gaze (as *charm person*) to charm targets into picking it up and defending it. A charmed target is automatically hit by the raggedy man's gossamer thread attack. Raggedy men take no damage from blunt weapons.

Raggedy Man: HD 4; AC 2[17]; Atk slam (1d6) or gossamer strand (1d4 + life drain); **Move** 12; **Save** 13; **AL** C; **CL/XP** 5/240; **Special:** beguiling gaze (3/day, 30ft range, as *charm person*, save avoids, charmed target automatically hit by gossamer strand attack), gossamer strand (30ft ranged attack, inflicts life drain on next round), immune to blunt weapons, life drain (automatic 1d4 damage, raggedy man gains damage amount as hit points), vulnerable to fire (200% damage).

Tear Collector

Hit Dice: 6
Armor Class: 5[14]
Attack: corrosive touch (2d4)
Saving Throw: 11
Special: +1 or better magic weapons to hit, acid tears, immune to acid and fire
Move: 12/12 (swim)
Alignment: Chaos
Challenge Level/XP: 8/800

A tear collector is a humanoid-shaped creature chiseled from rock salt. The small creatures form from the tears of sadness spawned by tragedy or unintended consequences. A tear collector attacks with its corrosive touch. Three times per day, it can unleash a 15-foot cone of acidic tears that do 2d6 points of damage to all within range (or half as much with a successful saving throw). Magic weapons are required to hit a tear collector, and they are immune to acid and fire.

Tear Collector: HD 6; AC 5[14]; Atk corrosive touch (2d4); **Move** 12 (swim 12); **Save** 11; **AL** C; **CL/XP** 8/800; **Special:** +1 or better magic weapons to hit, acid tears (3/day, 15ft cone, 2d6 damage, save for half), immune to acid and fire.

Unrequited

Hit Dice: 6
Armor Class: 5[14]
Attack: baleful touch (1d8 + level drain)
Saving Throw: 11
Special: +1 or better magic weapons to hit, incorporeal, mournful glare, resistances (cold, electricity, and fire)
Move: 12/12 (fly)
Alignment: Chaos
Challenge Level/XP: 8/800

Unrequiteds are incorporeal beings that appear as wispy, crimson vapors but that can periodically take their original humanoid forms. They attack with a baleful touch that drains one level from a creature that fails a saving throw. Three times per day, an unrequited can turn its mournful glare on any creature within 60 feet. The target must make a saving throw or suffer a −1 penalty to attacks and saves and have its movement halved for 1d4+1 rounds. Magic weapons are required to hit an unrequited. Unrequiteds take half damage from cold, electricity, and fire.

Unrequited: HD 6; AC 5[14]; Atk baleful touch (1d8 + level drain); **Move** 12 (fly); **Save** 11; **AL** C; **CL/XP** 8/800; **Special:** +1 or better magic weapons to hit, level drain (1 level with touch, save avoids), incorporeal, mournful glare (1/day, 60ft radius, save or movement halved and −1 penalty to attacks and saves for 1d4+1 rounds), resistances (cold, electricity, fire) (50% damage).

Wahuapa (Maizefolk)

Hit Dice: 7
Armor Class: 7[12]
Attacks: 2 claws (1d6 + blood meal)
Saving Throw: 9
Special: blood meal, camouflage, entangle
Move: 9
Alignment: Neutrality
Number Encountered: 1 or 1d10
Challenge Level/XP: 8/800

Wahuapas (which are also known as maizefolk) are stalks of corn or maize that move on tendrilled, fibrous legs. One ear of maize at the top of the plant's central stalk seems to function as its crude brain, though the monstrosity lacks eyes, ears, or any other discernible sensory organ or orifice. They are often indistinguishable from normal stalks of corn or maize in which they hide (1-in-6 chance to spot if motionless). Wahuapas attack with their sharp, serrated leaves, which slash their opponents. If the target fails a saving throw, it takes an additional 1d4 points of damage. The wahuapa feasts on the spilled blood to heal itself (gaining hit points equal to the damage done). Three times per day, a wahuapa can cause plants to grow in a 10-foot radius within a 60-foot radius of the creature. A creature caught in the tangle of plants must make an Open Doors check to escape.

Wahuapa (Maizefolk): HD 7; AC 7[12]; Atk 2 claws (1d6 + blood meal); **Move** 9; **Save** 9; **AL** N; **CL/XP** 8/800; **Special:** blood meal (save or additional 1d4 damage, wahuapa gains hp equal to damage), camouflage (1-in-6 chance to spot while standing still in maizefield), entangle (3/day, plants grow in 10ft radius within 60ft range, save or restrained, Open Doors check to escape).

Wight, Sword

Hit Dice: 8
Armor Class: 5[14]
Attacks: bastard sword (1d8 + level drain) or slam (1d4 + level drain)
Saving Throw: 8
Special: +1 or better magic or silver weapons to hit, darkvision (60ft), level drain
Move: 9
Alignment: Chaos
Number Encountered: 1 or 2d10
Challenge Level/XP: 10/1,400

These wicked and depraved creatures lived and died by the sword, and now, their dark taint passes through their weapons to tear at your soul. Much like the standard wight, these undead abominations are warped and twisted caricatures of their former selves. The sword wight bears a massive bastard sword, and the cold touch of the grave courses through the creature, through the weapon, into the hapless target. If a sword wight hits an opponent with its bastard sword or touch, the victim must save or lose a level. Any human killed or completely drained of levels becomes a sword wight.

Sword Wight: HD 8; AC 5[14]; Atk bastard sword (1d8 + level drain) or slam (1d4 + level drain); **Move** 9; **Save** 8; **AL** C; **CL/XP** 10/1400; **Special:** +1 or better magic or silver weapons to hit, darkvision (60ft), level drain (1 level with hit, save avoids). **Equipment:** chainmail, bastard sword, gold and sapphire circlet (100 gp value).

Appendix B: New Items and Magic

The following items and magic are found in this adventure:

New Armor

Ichcahuipilli. This two-inch-thick light armor resembles a vest designed to protect the wearer's torso from the neck to the hips against arrows and sharp blades. It consists of layers of cotton and vegetable fiber stitched together in a network of interconnected diamond-shaped patterns and then soaked in brine or another saline solution to harden the materials.

Olli. Armor smiths combine latex and the juice from a morning glory vine to create a flexible and resilient material resembling modern rubber. Although typically used to create the tlatchli, clever innovators use the durable substance to protect warriors from injury. The lightweight suit includes a jacket and leggings. An inner and outer lining of breathable linen provides added comfort. While wearing this armor, you reduce any falling damage you take by 1d6 points, though you cannot reduce the falling damage below 0. Because it is made from plant-based products, druids are permitted to wear olli, and it is immune to rust.

Ollixalli. One day, Atoyapaca, an innovative botanist and renowned jeweler, heated olli and combined it with ground quartz to enhance its strength. His bold experiment exceeded his wildest expectations, leading others to follow in its footsteps by adding other silica-based and sulfurous components to the liquified olli mixture. The delicate and laborious process of creating ollixalli is a tightly guarded secret confined to those who have the technical expertise and specialized equipment required to set the ollixalli mold. Unlike conventional heavy armor, a suit of ollixalli consists of a lightweight jacket and pants that protect the torso and limbs. Ollixalli has no metal components, making it suitable for druids and immune to rust. Because of the specialized training and equipment needed to create ollixalli, the armor remains extremely expensive and rare.

Tehuatl Armor

Armor Type	Effect on AC from base 9[10]	Weight[1] (pounds)	Cost
Light Armor			
Ichcahuipilli	−1[+1]	4	15 gp
Medium Armor			
Olli	−4[+4]	12	75 gp
Heavy Armor			
Ollixalli	−5[+5]	25	1,000 gp

[1] Magical armor weighs half normal

New Weapons

Itztopilli. This axe has a wooden haft with a bronze head fitted into a groove built into the haft. The head is long and narrow, and its cutting surface is only slightly wider than the axe's flat back. The itztopilli's versatile design allows you to hack into flesh as well as chop wood with remarkable accuracy and comparable ease. Indeed, most woodworkers incorporate the weapon into a standard set of carpenter's tools.

Macuahuitl. Made from hardwood such as oak, this weapon resembles a long, flat paddle with obsidian or flint chips embedded into the weapon's edges. The insertion of these incredibly sharp stones gives the weapon unmatched cutting power at the cost of increased fragility. When you attack a creature with this weapon and roll a 19 or 20 on the attack roll, the weapon deals double damage. Furthermore, the creature struck loses 1d4 hit points each round due to the blade gouging a deep laceration through its flesh. The damage increases by 1d6 if you inflict another deep laceration during a subsequent attack.

However, when you attack a creature with this weapon and roll a 1, you damage the weapon. Your attacks with the weapon suffer a −1 to-hit penalty, and you can no longer inflict a deep laceration. If you damage an already damaged weapon, the weapon breaks, rendering it useless.

Tecpatl. Carved from flint or obsidian, this double-edged knife has a pointed tip and a decorative wooden, stone, or mosaic handle. Although an effective, close-quarters combat weapon, the tecpatl is predominately used in religious rites and revered for its multitude of symbolic roles. When used in battle, it may open a deep laceration in the same manner as described under the **macuahuitl** entry (see above). However, because the knife itself is made entirely of flint or obsidian, the weapon irreparably breaks instead of being damaged when you roll a 1 on your attack roll with the weapon.

Tehuatl Weapons

Weapon	Damage	Weight (pounds)	Cost
Melee Weapon			
Itztopilli	1d6	2	4 gp
Macuahuitl	1d8[1]	2	10 gp
Tecpatl	1d4[2]	1	2 gp

[1] Deals double damage on roll of 19–20; deep cut does 1d4 additional damage per round; second deep cut raises continual damage to 1d6; roll of 1 damages weapon and imposes −1 to-hit penalty; second roll of 1 destroys weapon

[2] Deals double damage on roll of 19–20; deep cut does 1d4 additional damage per round; second deep cut raises continual damage to 1d6; roll of 1 destroys weapon

New Equipment

Tlilitl. A creature that drinks this vial of vanilla-flavored liquid with hints of chocolate gains a +1 saving-throw bonus against magical sleep for one hour.

Magic Weapons

Stone of Stunning

Made from hard rubber, these spherical sling stones are designed to debilitate rather than kill an enemy. When the stone hits a creature, the target takes no damage but must succeed on a saving throw or be stunned for 1d4 rounds. Once a stone stuns a creature, it becomes nonmagical.

Miscellaneous Magical Items, Greater

Cuacalalatli of the Beast

These wooden helmets are shaped into the likenesses of various beast heads. The protective device fits over the head and covers the top and back of the skull as well as the jawline. Anyone wearing one of these helmets gains the animal's abilities. The type of beast associated with the helmet determines its specific properties:

Crocodile: The wearer can slam its target for 1d6 points of damage.

Eagle: The wearer cannot be surprised.

Frog: The wearer can hold his or her breath for 15 minutes and gains a +1 to-hit bonus when fighting underwater.

Jaguar: The wearer gains a +1 bonus to attacks and damage against injured foe.

Monkey: The wearer can scale vertical walls (Climb 9).

Serpent: The wearer can slide through gaps half his or her size.

Usable by fighters and thieves.

WAR PAINT

Typically stored in clay jars, each container holds 1d3 applications of viscous pigments made from dyes and other colorful components. A creature can wear no more than three different colors of paint at a time, and only one color of war paint can be applied to a weapon. Any attempt to apply more colors fails. Each application of paint lasts for one turn regardless of color. The *war paint's* color determines its effects:

Black: The wearer is infused with a dark energy that deals 1d6 points of damage to any creature touched or struck.

Blue: A frigid chill courses through the wearer's body and causes frost to form on any weapon. The cold is harmless to the wearer and the weapon. This cold deals an additional 1d6 points of damage with a successful strike.

Green: The wearer cannot be restrained or paralyzed.

Orange: The wearer is immune to fear.

Purple: The wearer gains a +1 to-hit bonus during combat.

Red: Warmth radiates through the wearer's skin and causes one weapon to glow red-hot. The heat is harmless to the wearer and the weapon. This fiery weapon deals an additional 1d6 points of fire damage.

White: The wearer's weapon deals an additional 1d6 points of damage to undead and fiends.

Yellow: Energy surges within the wearer's body and causes one weapon to crackle with electrical energy. The electricity is harmless to the wearer and the weapon. The weapon deals an additional 1d6 points of electrical damage.

Usable by all classes.

MISCELLANEOUS MAGICAL ITEMS, LESSER

TANGLED GOURD

This roughly spherical green, orange, or bright yellow gourd is three inches in diameter and weighs one pound. If thrown, the gourd rips apart on impact and fills the area with fibrous vines. Each creature within a 10-foot radius of where the gourd lands must succeed on a saving throw or be restrained by the vines. Creatures that enter the area must succeed on a saving throw to also avoid being restrained. Restrained creatures take 1d6 points of damage each round. A creature restrained by the vines can make an Open Doors check to escape. The effects last for 1d4 + 2 rounds. Usable by all classes.

Designation of Product Identity: The following items are hereby designated as Product Identity as provided in section 1(e) of the Open Game License: Any and all material or content that could be claimed as Product Identity pursuant to section 1(e), below, is hereby claimed as product identity, including but not limited to: **1.** The name "Frog God Games" as well as all logos and identifying marks of Frog God Games, LLC, including but not limited to the Frog God logo and the phrase "Adventures worth winning," as well as the trade dress of Frog God Games products; **2.** The product name "The Lost Lands," "Tehuatl", "Maize and Monsters" as well as any and all Frog God Games product names referenced in the work; **3.** All artwork, illustration, graphic design, maps, and cartography, including any text contained within such artwork, illustration, maps or cartography; **4.** The proper names, personality, descriptions and/or motivations of all artifacts, characters, races, countries, geographic locations, plane or planes of existence, gods, deities, events, magic items, organizations and/or groups unique to this book, but not their stat blocks or other game mechanic descriptions (if any), and also excluding any such names when they are included in monster, spell or feat names. **5.** Any other content previously designated as Product Identity is hereby designated as Product Identity and is used with permission and/or pursuant to license. This printing is done under version 1.0a of the Open Game License, below.

Notice of Open Game Content: This product contains Open Game Content, as defined in the Open Game License, below. Open Game Content may only be Used under and in terms of the Open Game License.

Designation of Open Game Content: Subject to the Product Identity Designation herein, the following material is designated as Open Game Content. (1) all monster statistics, descriptions of special abilities, and sentences including game mechanics such as die rolls, probabilities, and/or other material required to be open game content as part of the game rules, or previously released as Open Game Content, (2) all portions of spell descriptions that include rules-specific definitions of the effect of the spells, and all material previously released as Open Game Content, (3) all other descriptions of game-rule effects specifying die rolls or other mechanic features of the game, whether in traps, magic items, hazards, or anywhere else in the text, (4) all previously released Open Game Content, material required to be Open Game Content under the terms of the Open Game License, and public domain material anywhere in the text.

Use of Content from *The Tome of Horrors Complete*: This product contains or references content from *The Tome of Horrors Complete* and/or other monster *Tomes* by Frog God Games. Such content is used by permission and an abbreviated Section 15 entry has been approved. Citation to monsters from *The Tome of Horrors Complete* or other monster *Tomes* must be done by citation to that original work.

OPEN GAME LICENSE Version 1.0a The following text is the property of Wizards of the Coast, Inc. and is Copyright 2000 Wizards of the Coast, Inc. ("Wizards"). All Rights Reserved.

1. Definitions: (a) "Contributors" means the copyright and/or trademark owners who have contributed Open Game Content; (b) "Derivative Material" means copyrighted material including derivative works and translations (including into other computer languages), potation, modification, correction, addition, extension, upgrade, improvement, compilation, abridgment or other form in which an existing work may be recast, transformed or adapted; (c) "Distribute" means to reproduce, license, rent, lease, sell, broadcast, publicly display, transmit or otherwise distribute; (d) "Open Game Content" means the game mechanic and includes the methods, procedures, processes and routines to the extent such content does not embody the Product Identity and is an enhancement over the prior art and any additional content clearly identified as Open Game Content by the Contributor, and means any work covered by this License, including translations and derivative works under copyright law, but specifically excludes Product Identity; (e) "Product Identity" means product and product line names, logos and identifying marks including trade dress; artifacts; creatures; characters; stories, storylines, plots, thematic elements, dialogue, incidents, language, artwork, symbols, designs, depictions, likenesses, formats, poses, concepts, themes and graphic, photographic and other visual or audio representations; names and descriptions of characters, spells, enchantments, personalities, teams, personas, likenesses and special abilities; places, locations, environments, creatures, equipment, magical or supernatural abilities or effects, logos, symbols, or graphic designs; and any other trademark or registered trademark clearly identified as Product identity by the owner of the Product Identity, and which specifically excludes the Open Game Content; (f) "Trademark" means the logos, names, mark, sign, motto, designs that are used by a Contributor to identify itself or its products or the associated products contributed to the Open Game License by the Contributor; (g) "Use", "Used" or "Using" means to use, Distribute, copy, edit, format, modify, translate and otherwise create Derivative Material of Open Game Content; (h) "You" or "Your" means the licensee in terms of this agreement.

2. The License: This License applies to any Open Game Content that contains a notice indicating that the Open Game Content may only be Used under and in terms of this License. You must affix such a notice to any Open Game Content that you Use. No terms may be added to or subtracted from this License except as described by the License itself. No other terms or conditions may be applied to any Open Game Content distributed using this License.

3. Offer and Acceptance: By Using the Open Game Content You indicate Your acceptance of the terms of this License.

4. Grant and Consideration: In consideration for agreeing to use this License, the Contributors grant You a perpetual, worldwide, royalty-free, non-exclusive license with the exact terms of this License to Use, the Open Game Content.

5. Representation of Authority to Contribute: If You are contributing original material as Open Game Content, You represent that Your Contributions are Your original creation and/or You have sufficient rights to grant the rights conveyed by this License.

6. Notice of License Copyright: You must update the COPYRIGHT NOTICE portion of this License to include the exact text of the COPYRIGHT NOTICE of any Open Game Content You are copying, modifying or distributing, and You must add the title, the copyright date, and the copyright holder's name to the COPYRIGHT NOTICE of any original Open Game Content you Distribute.

7. Use of Product Identity: You agree not to Use any Product Identity, including as an indication as to compatibility, except as expressly licensed in another, independent Agreement with the owner of each element of that Product Identity. You agree not to indicate compatibility or co-adaptability with any Trademark or Registered Trademark in conjunction with a work containing Open Game Content except as expressly licensed in another, independent Agreement with the owner of such Trademark or Registered Trademark. The use of any Product Identity in Open Game Content does not constitute a challenge to the ownership of that Product Identity. The owner of any Product Identity used in Open Game Content shall retain all rights, title and interest in and to that Product Identity.

8. Identification: If you distribute Open Game Content You must clearly indicate which portions of the work that you are distributing are Open Game Content.

9. Updating the License: Wizards or its designated Agents may publish updated versions of this License. You may use any authorized version of this License to copy, modify and distribute any Open Game Content originally distributed under any version of this License.

10. Copy of this License: You MUST include a copy of this License with every copy of the Open Game Content You Distribute.

11. Use of Contributor Credits: You may not market or advertise the Open Game Content using the name of any Contributor unless You have written permission from the Contributor to do so.

12. Inability to Comply: If it is impossible for You to comply with any of the terms of this License with respect to some or all of the Open Game Content due to statute, judicial order, or governmental regulation then You may not Use any Open Game Material so affected.

13. Termination: This License will terminate automatically if You fail to comply with all terms herein and fail to cure such breach within 30 days of becoming aware of the breach. All sublicenses shall survive the termination of this License.

14. Reformation: If any provision of this License is held to be unenforceable, such provision shall be reformed only to the extent necessary to make it enforceable.

15. COPYRIGHT NOTICE

Open Game License v 1.0a Copyright 2000, Wizards of the Coast, Inc.

System Reference Document Copyright 2000, Wizards of the Coast, Inc.; Authors Jonathon Tweet, Monte Cook, Skip Williams, based on original mate-rial by E. Gary Gygax and Dave Arneson.

System Reference Document 5.0 Copyright 2016, Wizards of the Coast, Inc.; Authors Mike Mearls, Jeremy Crawford, Chris Perkins, Rodney Thompson, Peter Lee, James Wyatt, Robert J. Schwalb, Bruce R. Cordell, Chris Sims, and Steve Townshend, based on original material by E. Gary Gygax and Dave Arneson.

Swords & Wizardry Core Rules, Copyright 2008, Matthew J. Finch

Swords & Wizardry Complete Rules, Copyright 2010, Matthew J. Finch

The Tome of Horrors Complete. Copyright 2011, Necromancer Games, Inc., published and distributed by Frog God Games; Author Scott Greene, based on original material by Gary Gygax.

Tome of Horrors Swords & Wizardry Update © 2018, Frog God Games, LLC; Authors: Kevin Baase, Erica Balsley, John "Pexx" Barnhouse, Christopher Bishop, Casey Christofferson, Jim Collura, Andrea Costantini, Jayson 'Rocky' Gardner, Zach Glazar, Meghan Greene, Scott Greene, Lance Hawvermale, Travis Hawvermale, Ian S. Johnston, Bill Kenower, Patrick Lawinger,Rhiannon Louve, Ian McGarty, Edwin Nagy, James Patterson, Nathan Paul, Patrick N. Pilgrim, Clark Peterson, Anthony Pryor, Greg Ragland, Robert Schwalb, G. Scott Swift, Greg A. Vaughan, and Bill Webb.

Blood Vaults of Sister Alkava. © 2016 Open Design. Author: Bill Slavicsek.

The Clattering Keep. © 2017 Open Design. Author: Jon Sawatsky.

Demon Cults & Secret Societies for 5th Edition. © 2017 Open Design. Authors: Jeff Lee, Mike Welham, and Jon Sawatsky.

Firefalls of Ghoss. © 2018 Open Design LLC. Author: Jon Sawatsky.

The Lamassu's Secrets. © 2018 Open Design LLC. Author: Richard Green.

Midgard Heroes Handbook. © 2018 Open Design LLC; Authors: Chris Harris, Dan Dillon, Greg Marks, James Haeck, Jon Sawatsky, Michael Ohl, Richard Green, Rich Howard, Scott Carter, Shawn Merwin, and Wolfgang Baur.

Midgard Worldbook. Copyright © 2018 Open Design LLC. Authors: Wolfgang Baur, Dan Dillon, Richard Green, Jeff Grubb, Chris Harris, Brian Suskind, and Jon Sawatsky.

The Raven's Call 5th Edition © 2015 Open Design; Authors: Wolfgang Baur and Dan Dillon.

Tome of Beasts. © 2016 Open Design; Authors Chris Harris, Dan Dillon, Rodrigo Garcia Carmona, and Wolfgang Baur.

Warlock Part 1. Authors: Wolfgang Baur, Dan Dillon, Troy E. Taylor, Ben McFarland, Richard Green. © 2017 Open Design.

Warlock 2: Dread Magic. Authors: Wolfgang Baur, Dan Dillon, Jon Sawatsky, Richard Green. © 2017 Open Design.

Warlock 3: Undercity. Authors: James J. Haeck, Ben McFarland, Brian Suskind, Peter von Bleichert, Shawn Merwin. © 2018 Open Design.

Warlock 4: The Dragon Empire. Authors: Wolfgang Baur, Chris Harris, James J. Haeck, Jon Sawatsky, Jeremy Hochhalter, Brian Suskind. © 2018 Open Design.

Zobeck Gazetteer for 5th Edition. Copyright ©2018 Open Design LLC. Author: James Haeck.

Creature Codex. © 2018 Open Design LLC; Authors Wolfgang Baur, Dan Dillon, Richard Green, James Haeck, Chris Harris, Jeremy Hochhalter, James Introcaso, Chris Lockey, Shawn Merwin, and Jon Sawatsky.

Tome of Beasts. Copyright 2016, Open Design; Authors Chris Harris, Dan Dillon, Rodrigo Garcia Carmona, and Wolfgang Baur.

Maize and Monsters, © 2020, Frog God Games; Author Tom Knauss

www.ingramcontent.com/pod-product-compliance
Lightning Source LLC
Chambersburg PA
CBHW042109160726
48295CB00017B/1039